GUNSHOT TRAIL

GUNSHOT TRAIL

Nelson C. Nye

GUNSMOKE

This hardback edition 2009
by BBC Audiobooks Ltd
by arrangement with
Golden West Literary Agency

ISBN 978 1 408 46232 4

British Library Cataloguing in Publication Data available.

For
That Great Old Gal
Who Edits the Cowboy's Bible—
MA HOPKINS!

Printed and bound in Great Britain by
CPI Antony Rowe, Chippenham and Eastbourne

GUNSHOT TRAIL

CONTENTS

1

LUCK RUNS OUT

SIX WASTED YEARS were behind him. Six down-the-river-sold years that could not be retrieved. This crazy chase that had carried Clem Andros over forty-five hundred miles of fine-combed territory was ended—ended with the same bitter irony that had seen and watched it prosecuted. The gods could have their laugh. Dakota Krell was dead.

Upon the table by which Andros sat slack-muscled stood a bottle and a tumbler. On the wall beyond, a faded print leered down at him through the gloom of its fly-specked glass. Andros was tired of everything. It was two-fifteen when he got that message that Dakota Krell had stopped a knife in a barroom brawl across the Border. The bottle had been full then; now it was useless, empty. Six hours to kill a bottle! But Andros was not drunk.

He was, however, suddenly aware the room was hot. His clothes were clammy with sweat as he shoved away from the table, wheeling toward the window on legs that refused to wabble, driving through the clutch of this trapped heat with a sultry fury. An impatient jerk of his big, scarred hands sent the window rattling up, full open. Summer smell and town smell came in to mingle with the stuffy stench so typical of hotel rooms. Twilight's glow was leaving the hills. Soon the good clean black of night would come to hide the squalor of a town whose only excuse of being was the nearby Reservation.

Andros put his back to the window with a soft-breathed oath and drew the back of a hand across his forehead. That woman in the next room was bawling again; not easily nor loudly, but softly. A kind of choking sound as though what she cried about hurt her.

San Carlos was no metropolis. It boasted one hotel—this one. Heat came through its warped board walls. In the wall that was nearest the woman light filtered through those

5

places where the boards no longer met. "I'll be back in about ten minutes," a man's rough voice said irritably. "Be ready."

Andros heard the floorboards creak beneath the fellow's boot heels; and then the door slammed loudly.

Andros shrugged his shoulders. No affair of his. Crying, he had noticed, came easily after marriage. Kind of seemed a natural sequence. Some women took a deal of pleasure in the business. He thought the woman yonder might quite likely be of that sort.

He walked stiff-legged across the room and stood by the table grimly. He was not old, but he was not young if you put any store in faces. Experience had carved harsh lines across this lean man's countenance. Sun and the winds had darkened it, toughened it like old leather. Wrinkles were graven about his eyes which, brightly, intently blue, were bleak and cold as gun steel.

He picked up the half-full glass on the table. He eyed it, morosely considering those wasted years. There were people he supposed, who would not consider them wasted. They had brought him distinction, certainly. All up and down the twisting length of this hell-bent border country men had learned to hide their feelings, to pick their way with caution, with their hands, plainly empty, in sight when chance brought him into their presence.

It was a distinction in which he took no pride. It was to him as shameful as the fawning manner and white-faced smirks of sundry belly-crawling sidewinders with whom he'd been forced to deal.

His life these years had not been pleasant. Clues to Dakota Krell's whereabouts had not been tacked to the public sign-posts. The trail had been a hard one; it had thrown him into company with this country's roughest breed.

He had survived.

Contemplation of that fact put saturnine creases at the corners of his eyes. Yes—he had survived.

"Black" Andros they had called him, though whether because of his clothes or deed, he had no means of knowing. Some had packed him quarrels, all neatly stage-managed, that later they might boast of having "downed" this "king of killers." These had not "quarreled" twice.

His big shoulders lifted in restless movement. He sloshed the untouched liquor in his glass, watching how it clung with

6

an oily sleekness. With a scowl he put it back on the table.

Need of action raked him. All his nerves were screaming and that hogwash in the tumbler had no further power to relax them. He had tramped this room till he knew every crack—and *that* had not helped, either. He had need of physical, *violent* action; every sinew and muscle ached. He had to have an outlet.

His mind kept sliding into the past. There was no "ahead" for Black Clem Andros. Everything lay behind. Six years of trail dust, trickery and hate. Brush-running years of turmoil, of jerky, beans and rancid coffee; of the spat and whine of drygulch lead. Of toothpick peril—the Arkansaw kind! Pounding hoofs and choking dust; the interminable bawling of long-horned cattle thrown wet across the Border. Swinging ropes and sudden death. Murder, battle, swift oblivion. These were the things those years had accounted as his share.

And now, in one bare second of time, some fool's knife had made of those things a mockery.

The irony of it bit into him like acid.

He came erect with a smothered oath, quartering the room with heavy stride, the dying sun throwing a solid shadow against the yonder wall boards. Impulse stopped him abruptly and, as swift, he caught up his sun-greened hat, throwing open the hallway door and going through its aperture sideways.

Never before had he come within miles of this town. Chance of recognition should be anyways sixty-forty—forty no one would know him. He would do his tramping out of doors where God gave a man room to swing his legs.

He stepped into the street and checked his stride midpace. Dusk had settled, but light from the hotel windows showed four stolid, blanket-wrapped figures squatted shoulder to shoulder along the plank walk's edge. Indians. San Carlos Apaches from the Reservation. Sharp of eye and smooth of face. Short-worded, but long of memory.

He shoved his hands deep into his pockets and swung his head in a watchful arc, six years' care and vigilance breaking through the fog of his temper.

In that deeper black across the street a denser shape moved fractionally. Farther down, Andro's raking stare picked up another bit of movement; discerned the pin-point glow of a cigarette in the curdled gloom of a stable doorway. A fourth,

7

discovered among the gathered shadows of a cottonwood, sent sudden clamor through him.

Temper burned like a white flame in him and one swift step took him out of their sight beneath a wooden awning. He brought his fists from his pockets and stood there waiting for the play with his hand half curled in the darkness.

He had not long to wait.

Across the way a door swung abruptly open, its bar of light striking hungrily through the felted gloom of the dusty road. Andros saw the placed shapes stiffen as a man's big form, emerging, momentarily blocked the beam. Andros knew in that quick moment where the watcher's interest lay. His muscles loosed their tension.

But the next instant saw them stretched wire-taut again.

His chest and shoulders took a forward sloping while he called himself a fool—while he told himself what was going on here was none of his affair.

But he understood, even as he said it, what it was he had to do. The man silhouetted in that yonder doorway wore the uniform of the newly-established Forest Service. He stood for law and order—something this country had been a long time needing.

Perhaps it was ironic that a man who for six years, people said, had been doggedly bucking all kinds of law should take time out to feel kinship with it now. But Andros knew what would swiftly happen the second that Ranger left the doorway. Those men had not been posted there to while away the time.

He knew the total brashness of this thing he was about to do—the fleeting, bitter quirk of his lips showed that. But it did not stop him. He raised his voice and yelled: "Get back! Get back inside that house!"

The echoes of it slammed the street's false fronts, fell, and dimmed away. A deep stillness settled, through which he plainly heard the emboldened voices of night insects. Nothing else. The Ranger was gone from the doorway. The waiting shapes were also gone.

Andros looked across at the Indians. Their stolid forms still showed against the light from the hotel windows. They hardly seemed to have moved an inch, hunched shoulder touching hunched shoulder. They cared for no part in the white man's medicine.

It was a cunning wisdom. No one but a fool bought chips in a game that didn't concern him. It was Black Clem Andros' weakness—a soft streak in him. A thing he had constantly fought against, yet had been unable to conquer. Like enough it would bring him to an early grave, if his enemies' guns or a hangman's noose didn't take care of him earlier.

He shrugged. Straightening, he turned his steps toward the lights of a saloon that, up the street a little way, winked out at him invitingly. But, nearly there, he changed his mind and dragged his spurs back to a restaurant.

He slipped swiftly in and got his back hard against a wall. Then he had his look around.

A constant thing, this watchfulness of surroundings; a steadfast habit born of turbulence and grown unbreakable as the habit of taking nourishment. It was one of those things which spelled the difference between continued living and six feet of earth. With Andros, there was always the chance of recognition, and what such awareness brought in its wake. He had many enemies, not all of whom he knew. He found it well to stay prepared.

It was a bit past time for evening meals and the place was almost deserted. Not counting himself there were only three customers present. A little Mexican, folded above his plate, was stowing food noisily. Yonder at a wallside table sat a man and a woman. The woman's glance stayed rigidly on her plate; by the plate's appearance she'd been doing little more than half-heartedly sampling the heaped-up portions presented by the establishment. Her companion's plate was nearly empty. He seemed to be muttering under his breath, and kept eyeing the woman darkly.

Andros took the table next to them and chose a chair that backed to the wall. The fat proprietor waddled up, got his order and departed. With his tarnished fork Andros made meaningless ruts in the table's spotted cloth. He was not particularly hungry. Habit was what had brought him here. All his reflexes were habit; though he could remember many times when he'd wanted nothing so much as to tuck his legs under a table and keep them there till he could hold no more. This was not such a time. He had come to eat because only God knew when he'd have the leisure to do it again.

Then his hard lips twisted as he recollected. Odd how difficult it was to break yourself of habit. There was no longer any reason why he should not eat when he felt like it. The chase was ended. Old habits and associations, like old shifts with their multiple dangers, belonged to the past. This was A.D.—time he was finding new purpose, new meaning to this life. Old ties no longer bound. Life seemed queer . . . a little empty.

His eyes strayed frequently to the couple at the adjoining table, remaining longest on the woman. He guessed it was the odd pallor of her face that attracted his attention—that, and the redness of her doggedly downfocused stare. Looked like she'd been crying.

He gave her a taciturn interest. She was not a woman really; just a girl, he thought, hardly out of her teens. Her tousled hair was fine-spun gold; like burnished bronze it gleamed in the lamps' mellow glow and Andros felt an urge to thrust his fingers through it. The richness of that golden hair gave her brown and willful eyes an added touch of piquancy. She was slender, pretty and golden, with lips of berry redness and a skin that gleamed like ivory and was smooth as bolted satin.

She was dressed in a ruffled white waist and blue riding skirt. Below the roundness of her chin a golden throat curved softly to the lacey collar of her waist, a covering that did little to hide the alluring contour of pointed breasts and the lithe, slim form beneath.

She must have sensed his covert study for her eyes came suddenly up at him and remained upon him searchingly. There was a strong curiosity in them and, briefly, an approval. There was intentness in that look, and a kind of troubled challenge. Then her long-lashed lids slipped down demurely and Andros, strangely disturbed, vigorously attacked the food that had been set before him.

He wondered idly if she were the one whose sobs he had heard in the hotel. She did not look like the crying kind. But a fellow never knew. Women were creatures set apart with different rules for conduct. No man could understand them, and would be a fool to try.

He was reaching for his pie when it happened. The man had said something to her, something gruff that Andros didn't catch. The girl spoke back, and he knew she was the one whose crying had annoyed him. But she had spunk; she said

10

distinctly, *"I won't!* I won't go there with you, Joce Latham, and you can't—"

The man, a tinhorn by his look and garb, showed experience in the handling of women. He wasted no words. He leaned above the table and slapped her soundly across the face.

She came to her feet with a little cry, her white cheek red with the print of his hand. Eye to eye they glared across the table, the girl pale, shaken, but still defiant; the man bent forward with a poised and threatening stiffness, a sultry anger bright in his gaze.

This was the way they were when Andros spoke. He said, very softly: "Don't reckon I'd undertake to do that any more, if I was you."

The gambler's shape swung completely round. Color livened the set of his cheeks and brash thoughts gleamed in his narrowed stare. His right hand dropped till its spraddled fingers were but half an inch from the gun that showed beneath the flung-back skirt of his coat. "Get out!" he growled with a husky slowness. *"Git!"*

He started ominously forward. Andros made no move. His soft laugh mocked the gambler's look. Latham stopped in his tracks, eyes gone bright with quick suspicion. "What the bloody hell you laughin' at?"

"You," murmured Andros, and laughed again. "You're not scarin' nobody."

A curse jarred out of Latham's teeth and his striking fingers closed about his gun. Detonation shook the walls of the place and the glint of the gambler's pistol skittered across three feet of floor. He crouched there, staring incredulously, eyeing the tingling fingers of his shocked and empty hand.

"You owe the lady an apology," Andros said, and suggestively added: "She's waitin'."

Latham's look got wild and black. He dug a knife from some place.

That was all Clem Andros needed. He let temper have its way with him. He took one forward step and struck. The blow took Latham below the ear and smashed him, gagging, against the wall.

Andros watched him, breathing heavily.

A dusty voice said at Andros' shoulder, "I guess you better come with me."

2

THE MAJOR MUST BE JOKING

SLOWLY TURNING, Andros saw a grim-faced man surveying
him. There was a pistol in this fellow's hand and the lamp's
light winked from the badge on his shirt.

With a shrug Andros said, "All right, Marshal," and, with
a bow for the girl, he scooped up his hat and walked to the
door. He paused there, waiting, wondering why the star-packer
hadn't asked for his gun.

He could feel the pull of the girl's watching eyes, but he
did not look her way again. It made no difference to him if
she were Latham's wife or something else which he didn't
label. It had been more the curse of his turbulent temper than
interest in her that had bought him chips. There was no
niche for a woman in the life of Black Clem Andros. If she
were anxious to get shut of Latham she had her opportunity.

But her voice came to him softly, turning him against his
will. He saw how her red lips smiled at him; nothing public
or blatant, but a smile his kind of man would not miss. The
curiosity was still in her eyes; the challenge was still there,
too, and some other thing which he did not scan too closely.

"I'd like to thank you," she said; and her voice was like
herself, desirable. "Not many men," she said quickly, "would
have had the courage to brace Joce Latham; and I want you to
know I appreciate it. I wouldn't have had it . . ." She broke
off, her glance swinging toward the marshal. "Perhaps I—" ·

" 'Fraid not, Miz Latham," the marshal said gruffly. "I
don't guess there's anything you can do about it." He looked
at Andros and nodded his head at the door.

"Don't you want my guns?" Andros said.

"I expect you can tote 'em, can't you?"

Andros' glance narrowed thoughtfully. "I ain't wantin' any
of that *ley del fuego* stuff."

The lawman met his challenging glance and the line of his
lips curled derisively. "Let's go," he said, and tilted his sixgun suggestively.

After the door had closed behind them and they'd gone some thirty paces, Andros asked his captor bluntly if he were to consider himself under arrest.

They had continued for several silent steps before the marshal answered.

Squirting out some of his drown-tobacco then, he cleared his throat. "That depends. For a *hombre malo* you sure are long on the chin music. Now you just mosey over towards that yonder cottonwood there, an' don't bother advertisin' yourself by walkin' through the light.

Arrived at the cottonwood Andros awaited the next move. The starpacker squinted round as though he were considering. "Just keep right on," he muttered, "till you come to that vacant lot."

Andros did. At the vacant lot the marshal directed, "We'll cut on over to the other side now—an' mind you steer clear of them lights."

"What is this," Andros growled, "a parade?"

"I'll tell you. There's some fellas in this town that ain't got sufficient savvy to shake hay. They got plenty o' curiosity though. I ain't figurin' to advertise my business. Cut on over now an' step lively."

The dark section of roadway having been crossed without incident the marshal, pressing close, said: "If it's all the same to you, we'll just turn down along this buildin'. Sort of snake along, Mister, an' when you reach the back, turn left."

Andros completed the maneuver, feeling strangely like a fool. Pausing obediently at his director's sibilant *"Psst!"* he waited while that cautious gentleman came alongside.

"See them stairs?" the marshal asked with his voice hauled down to a whisper. "Well, up at the top o' them is where we're headed for. Looks like we've give them fellas the slip—but I'm not takin' any chances. Keep quiet now. Shove ahead an' mind your step."

Major Cass Bocart, the Forest Supervisor if the prospective Tonto National Forest became an established fact, was close to fifty. He had a fighting jaw, a cold blue eye. One look sufficed to show a man his silver hair was not attributable to age; more like to be a memento, you'd say, of some of those occasions which had graved those deep-creased lines in his ruddy face. And you'd have been right.

13

Bocart had been selected for this post at that time last year when Theodore Roosevelt had kicked the legislature into action about the need for water in this country. He had proposed setting aside this vast Salt River watershed as a National Forest. That it had not yet been so proclaimed was the fault of neither the Major nor the President; both were fighting for it tooth and nail.

The Major's face, as he sat before his battered desk, was couched in somber lines. Big teeth champed savagely at his pipestem and the lips that curled about them were as tightly grim as his thoughts. He was bucking a stiff proposition; none realized it better than himself.

"Come in," he growled to a sudden knock, and lowered one hand beneath the desk's edge.

A tall and black-clad man came in and stood with a poised directness that took into account with one sweeping glance every detail of the room. The marshal, coming in behind him, closed the door and, eyeing Major Bocart sourly, said, "I see you got the shades drawed. Guess you ain't so hard as you put on to be. You want I should stick around?"

"What for, Tom? You reckon I'll be needing assistance?" The Major's eyes showed a fleeting twinkle. "Rather have you circulate. Like to keep that badge in people's minds."

The marshal spat at a knothole. "This fella," he said, "has been doin' his best t' commit suicide. You recollect Joce Latham, don't you? Well, this guy just busted hell out of him." He turned to the door, spoke over his shoulder: "Kinda figured you'd want to see him." He went on out. The door closed softly.

Settling back in his chair the Major folded burly arms across his chest and regarded the stranger frankly. He saw a black-haired man with a dark, burnt skin pulled tight across high cheekbones. The man's eyes were like smoky sage, indeterminate of hue but alive with a hard skepticism he did not bother to conceal. Tight-pressed lips cleaved this fellow's face above a coldly saturnine jaw, and the hat shoved back from his forehead was of the horsethief type, battered, faded. The whole look of him patterned on that hat and the Major, shrewdly studying him, decided this appearance was no paraded toughness but a thing very much a part of him—as real as the guns in the thick black belt that was buckled about his hips.

14

There was weight in this man. But it was a distributed weight, carefully balanced and obscured along the broad flats of his shoulders, in the sinews of his chest and arms. There was an unsmiling coldness in the directness of his regard; yet the Major slowly nodded, entirely pleased with what he saw.

"So you been bracing Latham, have you?"

The man took the time to turn those few words over, but he gave no answer to them. "First time," he said, "I ever heard of the Service walkin' in on a private quarrel. Must be plumb hard-up for trouble."

"Plumb hard-up," the Major admitted, "but not, by God, for trouble. I got more of that than I can handle. Sort of a stranger round here, ain't you?"

The black-clad man didn't answer.

The Major tried another tack. "Familiar with the Four Peaks country?"

"I've been there. Am I supposed to be under arrest?"

"You wouldn't be hunting for a job, would you?"

"First things first. I'm interested right now in findin' out where I stand." The shape of his cheeks changed slightly. "If I'm under arrest I want to know it. If I ain't I'll be sayin' goodnight to you."

"You're not if you take this job," Bocart said.

"Like that, eh?"

The Major smiled. "Are you taking it?"

The stranger said, "I'm not a fountain-pen man, Mister."

"The job I've got in mind don't call for any fountain pen." Major Bocart poked tobacco into his pipe with a stubby finger. He struck a match. He drew the flame down into the bowl of his pipe with a noisy sucking sound. He exhaled a gust of smoke, then said. "This job calls for a lot of nerve. And lead," he added softly. "I want a man who can use his think-box; who can put his lead where it will do some good."

The stranger grinned. "An' you think I fit that description?"

"It'll be no bed of roses," the Major said as though the man had accepted. "You'll need a lot of luck to cut it. But—"

"I didn't say I was interested—"

"You will be. And you're going to take it—"

"What is this job you keep harpin' on?"

"Undercover work." Major Cass Bocart said frankly: "No glory and no credit. If you slip, we don't even know you. If

15

you get in a jam you'll have to get yourself out. You'll be on your own without backing. The pay is good, but your biggest compensation—if you're the kind of man I think you are—will lie in the satisfaction of seeing a worthwhile chore done to the best of—"

"Brother Jones," the stranger drawled, "will pass around the plate."

Major Bocart scrubbed his jaw and grinned a little sheepishly. "Just the same—"

"The floral offering is received with thanks. Let's get down to brass tacks now."

The Major gave him one quick sharp look then turned his glance to the ceiling. For several moments he puffed in a reflective silence. Then he said, "The situation's this. Here in Arizona—in New Mexico, too, far as that goes—a number of usually antagonistic interests have lately amalgamated to put a stop to the creation of further Forest Reserves. This combine is a powerful one; it's made up of sheepmen, the big cattle kings, the lumber and railroad interests—it's got a hell of a lot of influence. You can easy see what more Forest Reserves will spell to the last two. To the stockmen such reserves are an even greater danger when considered in the light of present range methods. It is claimed they'll bring about the end of the open range—no more free grass, in other words. Neither sheep nor cattle will want to see that. They thrive on the present feudal system where might is all that's necessary to insure a lot of profit.

"Chief Forester Pinchot claims sheep are destructive to grass; he's pulling strings to get them barred from the preserves. Sheep need a lot of territory; they've got it now and they mean to keep it. The sheep kings work on a hundred per cent profit. They don't want to *buy* range so they're fighting us for all they're worth.

"The Combine's doing a deal of lobbying up in Washington; greasing palms and that kind of rinkydink. But the President's got his eyes open. He's lived out here. He knows that if present conditions are allowed to continue another five years the farmers and small ranchers haven't a snowball's chance in hell; Teddy knows they'll be put out of business by the capital back of sheep and beef. Forest Reserves won't ruin the big fellows —they've plenty of cash to buy range; but Reserves will save

16

the small independents. The only thing that *will* save 'em—"

"Very interesting. But what's all this got to do with me?"

"I'm getting there. All this fighting ain't being done at the Capitol. The worst of it's going on right here in Arizona. And, bad as it's been, what's happened already won't hold a patch—"

"Suppose," the stranger drawled, "you get down to plain facts. It ain't my habit to go into things blind. I'll want a few names an' figures."

Bocart nodded. "You'll get 'em when you give me the word—and when I'm convinced you're the man I want. So far you haven't said you'll take the job. Been a rancher, haven't you?"

"I've run cattle."

The Major looked at him shrewdly. "You've got the look of a Texas man. How many folks on your backtrail?"

There was a visible temper about this dark stranger that gave, the Major had noted, a certain color to his ironies. But his look had undergone a change; was stiff now and darkly inscrutable. "I guess," he drawled, "you better leave that to God an' me."

Poking the dottle in his pipe the Major struck another match, put a cloud of smoke about him. He said, speaking through it, "Do you want this job or don't you?"

"I'll reserve my say till I've heard the rest—till I've seen a few of your facts."

"For a brash looking man you're pretty cautious."

"Not cautious. Say rather I'm not in the habit of playin' things blind—"

"You'll be playing this blind regardless of how much I tell you," the Major said sharply. "I don't have half the facts myself. That's one of the reasons I need you. I can say this much—these sheepmen and their allies are prepared to go the limit. They mean to control that Four Peaks country and all the range above it. They don't want it made National Forest—" He broke off. "If you're hard enough to suit my book I'll confide a little more."

"Did you say *hard?*"

"I did." The Major got to his feet. "I've got to be damn sure of you, Mister. You've got to be bold to cut this."

He lifted a big Colt pistol from the drawer and stood with it in his hand, eyeing the stranger closely.

"Shoot if you must," that gentleman said, and the look of his grin was like granite.

But the Major's face stayed sober.

"You're pretty proud," he observed. "But how are your guts? Have you got enough for this?" He laid his pipe down carefully. His stare was bright as he explained with an added dryness. "The tests of the man I'm looking for, all other considerations satisfied, is simple. I take all the cartridges out of this cylinder but one—like this," he murmured, shaking four out and standing them up on the desk top. "Since there were only five in it to start with, that leaves one still ready for firing. The applicant for this little chore of mine picks up the pistol, puts its muzzle against his right temple, spins the cylinder and pulls the trigger."

He held out the gun, butt forward.

3

"YOU PREPARED TO BET ON THAT?"

THE STRANGER'S glance was very bright.

"Your gall should take you far," he said. "Put a loaded pistol to your head an' pull the trigger, eh? Think you'll find a man fool enough to do it?"

"I've found two. Unfortunately, both times the hammer dropped on the loaded chamber."

The room got very still. These two men looked each other over while locust sound in the night outside rose three full shades in loudness. The stranger's eyes were steely slits. His interest was cold and wicked.

"I'm wonderin'," he said, "why you haven't taken on the job yourself. Man with the kind of stuff runs in *your* veins—"

"I wish the hell I *could!*" Bocart said. "I'd take it in a minute!" The flash of his eyes showed a grim regret. "I'm too well known in this country. Can't hardly waggle my elbow without the length of Salt River knows it. Sheepmen's spies're every place. Why, only tonight—but no matter. Man who handles this can't have any connection with the Forest movement. And a set of cast iron guts is only the first requirement of such a man."

Leaning forward the stranger put the flats of his hands whitely upon the desk. "I can savvy that part all right. But how can you tell but what *I'm* one of these sheepmen's agents?"

The Major's eyes were brightly cool. "I can't. That's one of the reasons for this gun trick. Red Hat's men are tough, but not *that* tough I imagine." Again he held the pistol out. "Well?"

The man grinned bleakly. "You've a rare persuasion, Major." He accepted the proffered gun, stood turning it over in his hands, professionally hefting its balance. "Nice taste in sixshooters. This your iron?"

"It was the pistol packed by the last man I tried to hire for this job." The Major knocked the dottle from his pipe, stood eyeing for a moment the few flakes of half-burned tobacco still clinging to its bowl. "It's yours . . . if you get the job."

A remote smile briefly curved the set of the stranger's lips. He twirled the gun by its trigger guard. "All right," he said, "I'll call you on that," and put the gun to his head.

No muscle of that lean hard body rippled as he met the Major's eyes. His own were cold as gun steel. Without blinking he lifted his left hand leisurely and twirled the weapon's cylinder. With a devil-may-care derision he set his finger to the trigger. The hammer clicked back with a loud, clear sound.

And then the hammer fell.

The Major's breath was a quick-drawn thing across that brittle stillness. He said abruptly, "I congratulate you," and bending, shoved the drawer shut.

The stranger returned the four removed cartridges to the emptied chambers of the pistol. He put the pistol in the waistband of his trousers. "Let's hear the facts," he said.

The Major's probing eyes were bright. He shoved a hand through his silver hair and a queer consideration darkly tightened the line of his mouth. "The Combine," he said rather gruffly, "is not satisfied merely to block the proposed extension of Forest Reserves; their lobbyists are prepared to filibuster all suggested changes to the present grazing laws. Pinchot, as I've said, is trying hard to get sheep barred from the Forests; that's one of the changes they'll probably get shelved. Meantime the Combine is maliciously set on getting more and more territory set aside for the use of sheep. This, with them, is a protective measure, just in case the bill gets by them. The easiest way to make land sheep range is by way of showing a previous use, by sheep, of such ground as they wish to take over. This way, of course, means gun-trigger trouble, but a few dead men mean nothing to them; they've been hard at it ever since they discovered our intentions with regard to this Salt River watershed. This long drought and the Combine together have just about spelled finish to the small rancher in this region. Those who've had the courage to fight back have pretty near all got the worst of it. They've been shot, they've been jailed and they've been lynched. This Combine," he reminded dryly, "represents real capital."

"I haven't heard any names. Ain't you got any idea who's back of it?"

Bocart nodded. "To mention a few, this Joce Latham you just tangled with is representing the town men of Long Rope; he's also repping for the lumber interests. He runs the biggest saloon and gambling dive in the country and bosses most of the tough-hombre gentry. We haven't been able to uncover, so far, the man who's watching the railroad's ante. Nor the cattle crowd's man. The sheep trusts are backing Talmage Vargas, better known as 'Red Hat.' "

"No big spreads in that Four Peaks country?"

"Only one—the Half-Circle Arrow. Operated by a man named Barstow. You'll meet him."

The Major let several moments pass while he puffed in a thoughtful silence. "I'm going to leave things pretty much up to you as to how you handle this. You'll have to decide for yourself what steps you can or can't take. I want the small ranchers protected and I want that bunch of plug-uglies cleaned out of Long Rope. That's about all for the moment, I guess."

The stranger was inspecting his calloused palms and said nothing.

"Here," the Major went on, removing a roll of bills from his desk, "is some expense money. Use it," he said, smiling wryly, "any way you see fit. Now aside from what we want accomplished, there's just one fact for you to bear in mind. Any jam you may get into is your tough luck so far as this

Service is concerned. Is that clear? Good. What name do you care to go by?"

"I've always used my own," he said. "Just write 'Clem Andros' in your book." And the smile he showed the Major's stare was a thin, cold thing; and sudden. " 'Black' Andros, if you prefer."

"Black Andros!" the Major cried, and jaw agape stood staring. He blinked and took another look. "Black Andros!" He repeated the name amazedly and shook his head dumbfounded. "That's a hard thing to believe, sir. . . . And yet—" He pulled himself together. "Some of the tales—"

"Yeah. I expect so—"

"But we've thought of Andros as a younger man—"

"How old do you think I am?"

"I'd say thirty, anyway."

"I'm twenty-three," Clem Andros said; and the way he said it settled it so far as the Major was concerned.

"By grab," he said, "I couldn't name a man I'd rather have, boy! With a rep like yours you're cut to order. No one will ever think to connect *you* with this Department!"

Color flashed suddenly through his cheeks and he said hastily: "What I mean is—"

"I expect I could guess. Don't—" Abruptly Andros stopped his talk. Head canted he seemed to listen to something beyond the Major's hearing. He was like that, standing stiff and off-balance, when a door behind him came violently open.

Three men slogged into the room with metal flashing in their hands; a fourth showed in the hallway's gathered gloom behind them.

The smell of sheep was acrid.

Bocart was never quite sure in his mind of just what happened after that. One moment Andros had his back to the door; the rest was a blue-smoked blur with Andros crouched above blazing guns. The smash of those two big pistols was a thunderous pulse in the room's jarred air.

Lamp flame swayed and shuddered. One man's hoarse scream went buffeting into the rafters. The tumultuous echoes slashed around long after the firing ceased.

Just inside the door were two crumpled shapes; across its sill another lay with yellow curls damp-plastered to its forehead. Down the hall's dark planks was a trail of blood.

"You'll do," Major Bocart said.

21

Sun's heat and furnace-driven wind had turned this Four Peaks country into a region bare as the desert. In the beds of long-dry washes sparse clumps of galleta grass showed, but these were but a mockery to the stark, lethargic cattle Andros saw from time to time. Waterholes were infrequent, and those he encountered gone dry as bone—as the bones that bleached the sands of the barren wastes about them. On more than one occasion he had distantly observed dismounted cowboys swinging axes in this killing heat; chopping down the tiny-leafed palo verdes while drearily ringed by a gaunted circle of lowing, wall-eyed cattle. These critters staggered up as though on stilts each time the thorny verdure fell. It must have been painful nourishment, but they followed the axe-swingers round like dogs.

Yet, grave though they were, it was not of the cowmen's troubles that Clem Andros now was thinking. His mind was fixed on the pistol he had got from Bocart, the gun inherited from the Major's second candidate. The one he had taken his test with.

It was a nickeled, long-barreled Colt's of forty-five caliber. It had bone grips inlaid with mother-of-pearl; a first-rate weapon of balanced weight and fine precision—as Andros had reason to know.

The gun had belonged to Dakota Krell.

Andros took it out and regarded it, in his eyes a morose glinting while his mouth was a tight-clamped slit. He presently put it away again, rolling it up in his slicker which he relashed behind his cantle. He rode then with his lambent gaze grim-searching his dun surroundings.

After awhile he was skirting a canyon's rim, toilfully climbing up into the uplands where the hot wind shouldered him roughly and the smell of scorched grass was a familiar, remembered bitterness.

A hundred feet below him, back down on the grassless plain, a rider was felling a giant sahuaro, stoic cattle indifferently watching him. The great thorny cactus toppled, bursting wide in the blistered wash. The cow brutes, gathered like stage props, dropped heads between bony spraddled legs to munch at the bitter pulp. Melon smell and the pungence of turnip drifted up on a gyrating dust devil.

With bitter thoughts Andros wiped streaks of sweat from his gritty cheeks and kneed the tired pony on again. Since noon

22

he had counted sixty carcasses; all that was keeping these cowmen going was such gruelling work as that below, a chore no self-respecting hand ordinarily would perform. Not a solitary calf, alive or dead, had Andros seen. He cursed, reflecting that there were none. If the sheepmen came this year it meant the end of these small cattlemen. If it had not been for sheep in the first place these punchers would not be having to chop cactus; there'd have been graze enough along these upper ranges to have carried these dying critters through.

Slanting sun dripped down like melted copper, throwing its final and fiery glow all across the land. The hush of desolation lay over the dust of this empty waste, gripping alike each skeletal spire, each gulch and bastioned rock-ribbed peak.

Long Rope was a huddle of bleached, false-fronted structures brooding in the dust of a gloomy gulch that cracked these timbered mountain flanks; eleven rude frames whipsawed from the neighboring pines and weathered to a drab and uniform gray. It included one hotel, one saloon replete with a grand miscellany of gambling devices and a trio of painted hussies still trading on the glories of a vanished past, one general store, a marshal's office, one stable and a blacksmith shop. All else was a sun-warped clutter of glassless windows with weeds and cactus growing up between the twisted planking of roofless porches. By daylight this was cow town, but with the falling of the sun other interests took it over and more upright men found it a place to keep away from.

It was dusk when Andros urged his pony up its wide and single street.

A seated man rose quietly from the hotel's shadowed veranda and faded through the door. By the blacksmith shop an idler cuffed his hat across sharp eyes and dropped one hand to his sagging belt. Night air pulsed a coolness down this street, acrid with the smell of the blacksmith's forge.

Andros' regard was quick and keen as he bent the gelding's course toward the stable and swung his head neither right nor left when a burly man rolled out of its doorway and gave him a stiffly searching look. Brief was that look and impatient was the gesture of this fellow's hand as, abruptly, he turned and vanished down an alleyway between two farther buildings.

Bleak humor touched Andros's wide thin lips. For this was history repeating itself as it had a thousand times during

23

his six-year hunt for the man-killer, Krell. He was being sized up. Later there would be further developments. These things made an unforgettable pattern and, though occasionally their sequence differed, were as familiar to Andros as the stitching in his boots.

He swung down before the stable and after some moments its proprietor came out. A slender, leather-faced man who yet lacked that definite gauntness so generally characterizing the men of this high region. He lighted a lantern he was carrying and carefully hung it from a hook above the doorway. Nothing in Andros' face gave away his cognizance of the motive that had swayed the man. Andros' face gave nothing away—not even when the stableman turned and casually bent, lifting one of the gelding's hoofs.

"How are the folks at Quinn River Crossing?"

Andros was curling himself a smoke when the man's soft words drifted up to him. His glance stayed on his building smoke till the cigarette was completed. His gaze came up then coldly, sharp on the stableman's countenance. He could not place the lean-bodied man. This was not strange for in six years of wanderings he had met a lot of such hombres.

But the man knew him—had known him instantly.

"I thought Dakota Krell was dead," he said.

And so Krell was, said Andros' mind; and saw in that tight moment what part he'd have to play in this town if he was to survive and aid the Forest Service. Only fear could serve him here—fear of his deadly guns. He could no longer hope to hide his identity; he was committed by this man's words to make the most of it. Quinn River Crossing was in north-western Nevada, within stone's throw of the Oregon line. If a man from that far place were here and recognized him, there might be others here from other places. And these would also recognize him. Once seen, Andros was not a man to be forgotten.

He stared at the stableman gravely. "I'll be stoppin' here a spell," he said, and walked away.

Where the saloon's bright lamps cut a bold path through the gathered murk and spilled their gold across a restive line of racked range horses, a group of men had gathered.

Andros turned that way.

Approaching, he observed two central figures plainly; these

24

were the dominant factors in that group. All others were merely watchers.

He came to a pause by the edge of this group, stopping by a pot-bellied man. Light from the nearby windows showed the two principals clearly. One, a confident, swaggering fellow, stood baiting a person half his size, and by his look deriving a deal of satisfaction from the process.

Andros' wheeling shoulders abruptly stiffened and he went shoving through the group with a rude directness. There was a dark look in his cheeks as he came to a stop before the pair.

The slender person was a girl. The burly man laughed. "Hell," he scoffed, "you ain't got a waddy on your payroll with half enough salt to teach me—"

"You prepared to bet on that?" Andros murmured.

4

A MAN'S COLD WAY

THE BIG man turned with the quick, lithe speed of a cat. It was the first good look Andros had of his face. Under a low-crowned, wide-rimmed hat the fellow showed good features; a face probably thought very handsome by any number of impressionable women. Even Andros would have owned to the man's good looks at another time or place perhaps. He had black hair—black almost as Andros' own, and beneath the wide, cleft chin his hat straps were fastened through a silver concho. A second concho held the dangling ends of the lavender scarf pulled tight about his throat. His shirt was of gray flannel tucked into corduroy trousers. These were protected by chaps as scarred as Andros' black ones. Good range boots peeped from under them; range boots with silver spurs.

Yet plainly this was no cowboy.

About his heavy waist were strapped two sagging cartridge belts, scuffed and dark like their holsters. Pliable, well-oiled leather. Like the smooth and mellow ivory of his gun grips these told a story.

He had smooth cheeks that were sleek and suave and, just

now, a little critical. His derisive eye picked Andros over and he winked broadly at these avid watchers hemming them.

"Sorry, pilgrim—I'm a little hard of hearin'. Mebbe you better ride that trail again. Say it louder—"

"Is this loud enough?" Andros said; and, swaying forward, drove a smashing blow to the fellow's chin. The big man's head went rocking back and his bigger chest went rocking with it, and suddenly he found himself with his back in the yellow dust.

"You swivel-eyed snake!" he gritted. He got an elbow under him; hunched forward and got a knee beneath him and blurred a clawed hand beltward. Fast! Steel rasped leather and a bright flame tore from his thigh. Gun thunder jammed the street and rolled against the building fronts.

But Andros, experienced in the art, had flung himself aside. The big man's finger was clamping down for another shot when Andros' boot sent his pistol flying.

Andros' eyes were blazing slits. "You fool!" he said. "I ought to break that cutter across your head! Never throw a gun on me again—never! *Is that plain?*"

The man got up with his lips in a laugh. But he was breathing hard and the laugh did not match the look of his tawny eyes. "I expect it is," he answered. He backed up, bent, and retrieved his pistol. He shoved it back in his holster and stood a moment, tight-lipped, watching Andros darkly.

"I guess you're the Rockin' T ramrod—the *new* one," he said fleeringly. "Nothin' to get so proud about; she hires 'em reg'lar once a month an'—"

"Does she?" Andros said with a quick step toward him. Temper burned like flame in his eyes and the slant of his cheeks showed to what uncaring rashness the proper words might goad him. This was his weakness; this red rage-fog that, quick as a wink, could close his mind to danger. It was closed right now. He stopped with his chin a scant hand from the other man's. "You aimin' to insinuate somethin'?"

The twisted sneer got off the man's mouth. He found himself backing away from this stranger, moving with a foreign care, moving haltingly, step by cautious placed step until he felt his horse behind him. His left hand made a groping upward move for the horn. He revealed an extreme reluctance to remove his gaze from Andros' face.

"No." His voice was a curdled sound. "No," he said huskily;

"I guess not." He paused, big shoulders stiff, his gleaming eyes on Andros with a taut and straining watchfulness. "You're sittin' high an' feelin' proud. But it won't last—"

"Don't waste no dinero on that bet."

Andros' scarred brown fists hung loosely at his sides. "I gave you one warning. Here's another: Never let me catch you on range controlled by Rocking T."

He turned then, ignoring the man's malignant glance. To the girl he said, "Come on. If you got your shoppin' done it's time we was gettin' back."

That smooth he carried it off. He tossed one cool quick look around, noting its effect on the watchers' faces. Lamps' shine revealed their expressions stony.

The girl put a hand on his arm and her fingers closed on it tightly.

From his seat in the saddle the big man called: "I'll be rememberin' you!"

"I'd be some put out," Andros grinned, "if you didn't."

Night's meshed blue had thickened to a deeper shade and all these surrounding shadows had rushed together closely, crouching low like opaque walls, before the girl or Andros spoke. And then it was the girl, this belted boss of Rocking T, who broke their riding silence.

"You've made a bitter enemy," she said; and then her low voice stopped. It was strangely husky when she spoke again, suggestive of deep inner turmoil. "There are times when even the most sincere of thanks sound trifling—almost farcical. This is one of them. That man has bothered me before. You've done yourself no good by helping me. Grave Creek can nurse hate like an Apache."

Andros' eyes showed a grim amusement, but they sobered swiftly as he said, "He'll be more like to take his spite out on you, I'm scared."

"It's my quarrel though. You needn't have become mixed up in it."

"I'm in it now. Don't worry about me. Just count on me."

"But you don't understand what's back of this. That man is Grave Creek Charlie. He's boss of Red Hat's gun-throwing sheep crowd. They just about *run* this country," she said vehemently. "They moved in on us last year and, from the look of things, they're figuring to sift through here again."

He marveled at the low, gritty rasp of her quick-said words.

27

It was as though she hated these sheepmen personally; each nameless man of their outfit with a hard and gathered anger. He wondered what reason they might have given her for such bitter animosity. He wondered, but he did not ask.

He probed the night with a watchful interest. Summer's smell and greasewood's pungence came with the wind whipped off the desert. A late moon flung its argent haze across the black rim of yonder hills; and Andros rode without thinking, content with the night and pleased with the feeling of riding in this quiet girl's company.

The trail ahead was a vague ribbon gleaming through the murk of shadows. The stillness of vast distances was thick upon this country; the feel of it stirred him, renewed his strength and, someway, hope was reborn in him and some of the ingrained harshness of the past years fell away from him, and he rode with his head bowed, grateful.

Yet, after awhile, looking round he said, "A lonely land."

"But home to some of us," she answered. "To strangers it may not look like much—all they can see is the harshness, the barren bleakness of it. You have to live here to understand the worth of it. I couldn't begin to put it into words, but when you own a piece of the land your values change."

He nodded. How well he knew. "Ground gets in a fellow's blood," he said. "It's something tangible; something you can taste and smell and touch if you've got a mind to. Something a man can build hopes on. . . . A man that's got any," he added.

He rode then with his glance ahead, broad shoulders hunched a little as he thought of Dakota Krell whose gun was rolled in the slicker back of his cantle. He thought also of that Long Rope stableman who had known him at Quinn River Crossing. Some things didn't change, he told himself. They just grew scars and festered. Sometimes a man's past was like that. Looking back was not good medicine. If a man had a chore to do, he *did* it. He didn't stop to procrastinate, to count cost or a hundred other things—not if he was a *man*, he didn't. You had just one life to live. You lived it according to your lights.

He mused for quite a spell, gone moody, yet he did not think it queer to find himself beside this girl whom he hadn't known an hour ago—whose name he didn't know yet. That was all right; she didn't know his name, either. Perhaps if she

28

had he wouldn't be here. It was enough that he knew she owned a ranch; had been having foreman trouble.

He said with his shoulders twisting. "About that ramrod's job, ma'am . . . That Charlie pelican let on like you might be in need of a range boss. Might be I could fill—"

"The job," she said, "isn't open."

That was pretty plain. They rode without talk for another half hour, then Andros said abruptly: "Mebbe you could use an extra hand then. I could use the work—"

She said, not mincing words, "I haven't the money to hire anyone. I've four punchers working for nothing now, and a range boss, too, far as that goes. The punchers haven't drawn even smoking money for over six months. The Rocking T's got its back to the wall. If the sheep come through here again this year, you can have it for the taxes."

"Mebbe they won't come through—"

"They'll come." She said it hopelessly. There wasn't even a sob in her breath.

"What about the other outfits scattered through these hills? Reckon any of them would be hirin'?"

"No."

"Bad, eh?"

"Next year there won't be a cow critter in this country."

"What's happened to the cow crowd's guts? It use to be that a cattle spread would fight for its rights—"

"Fight!" In the moon's risen light he could sense the intensity of the look she flashed at him. He could not make out her features clearly nor catch their expression really; but the sound of her breath was expression enough—that and her stiff-set, back-thrown shoulders. Her words struck bitterly across the quiet.

"Listen! Last year sheep came through here. There wasn't much browse along the trails so the herders turned them up the hillsides, spreading them out. When they left, this range was stripped to the roots. Some of the ranchers got a little riled. They rode down into the sheep camps primed for trouble and ready to start it. The sheepmen palavered; they were slick with their lingo. And all the time the ranchers stood jawing the herders were pushing their sheep deeper into this country's best grass. It was too late to do much by the time we discovered it."

29

Andros rode for awhile, grim thinking.

"No," he said, "I guess talk never did solve much. There's some guys don't understand fair talkin'. Any of these Four Peaks ranchmen packin' irons?"

"They were packing irons last year." Her voice was choked with feeling. "Jack Broth killed a couple herders up on Tonto Creek. The sheep crowd pooled a lot of money and hired a lawyer to get Jack the limit. He got it. They sent him to Yuma and finally hung him."

The creak of riding gear, the clink of metal and the soft, steady drubbing of the ponies' hoofs were the only sounds to disturb a silence become physically uncomfortable.

Andros eyed the girl very briefly and turned his glance on the trail again. The girl had pluck—she had a lot of it. She had seen and felt the sheepmen's power, and like most others who had lately confronted it could find no weapon she could use against it. Bocart was right. They were going too far.

"What's happened to the calf crop?"

"There wasn't any."

"This drought?"

She shrugged. The bleakness of it held no hope. The cow crowd of the Four Peaks country were beaten—beaten badly, and they knew it. The prospect before them was one of ruin. They still hung on because it wasn't in a cowman's soul to ever quit; but they knew already what the end would be.

"You're pretty sure they're coming back—the sheep, I mean?"

"They bragged of it last year when ninety thousand sheep went north. Grave Creek boasted round they'd take the desert for a starter. Then, he said, they'd take over the good range up along the Verde. They took both. The only graze that's left this country that amounts to half a button is our higher range; the stuff we save for wintering. It's Grave Creek's brag they'll take that coming back."

"How about a deadline?"

There was no mirth in her brittle laughter. "Last year, we tried it three different places. Like slapping a bull between the horns."

"If they ain't stopped soon," Andros ventured, "looks like they'll gobble the whole of Arizona."

She said indifferently, "They'll gobble it. Most of these small ranchers round here have seen the Writing. They'd be glad to sell and get on out. But who'd be fool enough to buy?"

"The sheepmen might," Andros mentioned.

She said indignantly, "I'd rather give it back to the Indians! Even if they *could* the sheep crowd wouldn't buy. Why should they? You know well as I do all our graze is public domain. It's the start of every sheepman's argument—it's their God and Bible!" she said with her lips curled back.

The things discovered in her voice left Andros somber. Her outlook was so markedly like his own had been these last six years. Depressed, he rode with shoulders hunched, cheeks etched in moody lines of bitterness. These people knew too well what they were up against. The thought of it was defeating.

After awhile he said, "If you all bunched up and stood against them—"

"We've tried that, too. Barstow had that notion. He said if enough of us would get together on the thing the sheep crowd's legal machinery would jam. They convicted and hung Jack Broth, he claimed, because we had no organization. Together we could do something.

"It sounded good. We tried it. We met them at the river and we turned them back. But it wasn't any good. They crossed below. We had a little good beef left then and kind of figured to keep our eyes on it. But we found we couldn't watch every place."

Her voice had grown tired. She was weary. Her shoulders had a sag to them now and Andros felt conviction himself. But he wouldn't give in to it. Of course this was tough! It *had* to be tough to bother a man like Bocart.

"Ever try again?"

He saw her hat dip briefly. "We stopped another bunch ten days later. Grave Creek said we'd let him or he'd order camp right where he was and sheep that side clear to ledgerock. Barstow guessed mebbe it was better not to fight them."

"This Barstow," Andros said. "Who is he? Where does he come in?"

"Reb's the biggest rancher in these parts. He runs the Half-Circle Arrow—covers the whole far side of Diamond Mountain and spreads out north for twenty miles."

"Guess the sheep hit him pretty hard, eh?"

"They went around him."

Andros said: "Went around him, eh?" and after that a silence gathered. The girl seemed strangely embarrassed and just a little resentful. This displeasure became more marked when Andros suggested softly, "Didn't folks find that a little odd?"

"Why should they? He owns his own range; it's purchased, paid for, recorded. Reb's father was Constantine Barstow—the Pork King. The Half-Circle Arrow was a hobby with him; it is with Reb, far as that goes. He don't have to work for a living. He sided up through sympathy."

"I see," Andros said. "Kind of fancies playin' champion to underdogs. Expect he lent you men, eh? Lent you money too, I guess likely."

She eyed him sharply. She didn't reply immediately, and when she finally did there was reluctance in her voice.

"No-o-o . . ." She said it slowly, with her eyes straight ahead, and appeared to go on thinking.

Andros didn't. He said brusquely: "Advice, mebbe."

"Yes." She took a deep breath. "Yes!"

It was ten by the stars when, in a valley spread below them, Andros got his first clear look at the ranch headquarters of the Rocking T. Timbered hills hemmed its platter-like hollow and he nodded his head with approval. A well planned place —well built, too; and situated in such a way that winter winds must pass it by. The moon's blue slant struck silver sparkles from the eighty-foot tank between the house and the other buildings. All of these structures were made of logs long seasoned by the elements. Lamp's shine was a sheen on the bunkhouse windows. There was also a light in the ranchhouse, and Andros thought to catch a surprised look on the girl's stiff cheeks; then their ponies were taking them down to it swiftly.

The bunkhouse lamp winked suddenly out. Shadows stirred by its darkened front. A challenge ripped the pound of hoofs: "Who's there?"

The girl pulled up. Andros' horse stopped, too. Dust came up and touched his face. Suspicion was a stealthy feel in the dappled shadows of this waiting yard. There was a familiar something in the challenger's voice that evoked old scenes in Andros' mind; time-blurred, half-forgotten pictures, vague as the fragments pulled from a dream. He was not even certain if it was the voice itself or the intonation that jumped his mind back into the past.

With both hands rested across the pommel he sat unmoving, but his eyes were watchful.

The girl said, "It's all right, Sablon."

Ahead the shadows flattened out. A light came on in the bunkhouse. At a walk they put their ponies forward, the girl in the lead. She stopped by the porch. In the open door a man's still figure made a big and burly shape against the light. His lazy drawl reached Andros softly as he told the girl, "Was beginnin' to get a little worried about you—didn't have no trouble, did you?"

The girl said "No," and turned to Andros. They sat their saddles in the pooled gloom of the porch roof and neither could see the other's face with any clarity. Light from the man-blocked doorway did not touch them. Some walker's nearing progress scraped the flowing shadows back of them. She said: "You'll stay the night, at any rate. Since you're set on dumping your bedroll here I'll try and think up something. Thanks again for what you did. I'll talk with you in the morning."

The man who had followed them across the yard came up. It was the fellow, Sablon, who had challenged them. His half-remembered voice was gruff. "I'm wantin' to see you, ma'am. Right now. It's about that—"

"In the morning, Sablon—"

"No—right now. When I got something to say, I say it. I'm tellin' you now. Barstow better be hearin' this, too. We'll step in the—" He stopped abruptly, staring past the girl at Andros.

A cold suspicion thinned his words. "Who's that? What's *he* doin' here?"

Sablon's shape was stiff where he stood beside the girl's off stirrup. Through the dappled sway of foliage branches Andros saw his hand slide down and spread above his gun.

Her words striking out with a measured clarity, the girl began: "You may be rodding this outfit, Sablon—"

The man's rough voice plowed across her talk. Insistent, probing—like the feel of the peering eyes that stared from the shade of his hat brim.

"Who is he? We can't hev strangers round this spread. Them sheepmen got their spies—"

33

Andros said, very soft with his words, "Do I look like a sheep spy?" He swung down out of the saddle and stepped full into the moonlight. "I guess you know me, Cranston."

The sound of the man's shrill in-sucked breath was a plain thing in that stillness. The small pale blob of his poised gun hand gyrated nervously. It stiffened, rose a full six inches. His boots took him back three crunching steps.

The quiet increased, grew brittle. The man in the doorway lazily said, "What is this, anyway—some kind of play?"

Time was a nerve-strain plucking their sinews while wind made a down-draft and no one spoke.

Impatience lifted Andros' shoulders. His voice cut a cold lane through the shadows. "You're done here, Cranston. Pack your duffle."

The man-blocked doorway was suddenly empty. Light slopped out across the porch, its refracted radiance spreading like water, driving the dark back, showing the groupings of those stiff shapes. Each ear was strained for Cranston's answer. That it would come in gun flame no one doubted.

It did not come. The man left his gun deep-shoved in its holster, abruptly wheeling away with a curse. He crossed the yard with the lurching wallow of a man gone blind.

The other man reappeared in the doorway. "Come in—Come in," he muttered gruffly.

5

GUN PLAY

THEY MOUNTED the steps, the girl and Andros, and passed in with their dragging rowels cutting tinkles of sound from the frozen quiet. Tiredly the girl went up to the mantel, shucking her cartridge belt and pistol, placing them on the stone's cool surface by the faded picture of a gaunt old man.

She turned then. No expression blurred the pattern of her features. "I'm Flame Tarnell," she said; and her lifted brows put a question the rule of this land forbade her asking.

Flame! It suited her well, Andros thought; and had his

34

good long look at her then. Quickened interest roused his blood and rushed it through him turbulently, the challenging directness of her level glance disturbing the accustomed run of his thoughts.

He looked more closely.

Tall, she was, and slender—willowy. She was like some proud, commanding goddess. Her beauty was a vital thing, as real as this room or the other man's scowl. There was flame in every clean-etched inch of her as, impatiently, she waited his answer. Her eyes were the blue of surging oceans. The dark mass of her hair was black as midnight and her lips were the red of ripe crushed berries against the warm ivory of a flawless contour.

She stood poised, still asking her question; and, within him, Andros shrank from answering lest knowledge of his name and bruited repute change the look on her face to one of loathing. Temptation gripped him.

It was then the man spoke who had been in the doorway. His voice cut an easy slur through the quiet. To Flame he said: "You're wonderin' who this fellow is. A *man* could tell by lookin' at him. Just another drifter like that tinhorn, Sablon. I advise you not to have any truck with him. Easy come, easy go. I know his kind. He's got no interest in your troubles— all he's interested in's himself. You mark my words. He's a leather slapper. Keepin' him here will just promote more trouble."

Andros pulled his look from the girl reluctantly.

He turned a cold, quick-searching glance upon the speaker of those words.

The man was big. A solid looking hombre with the store clothes clinging snugly to his stocky, muscled figure. He made no move at Andros' turning; did not move the burly shoulders from their rest against the mantel. But his sleepy lids rolled slowly up, disclosing amber eyes whose measured glance in-differently brushed his own and turned back to the girl again as though the reaction of this man to what he'd said was of no import.

Andros said with a thin tranquility. "I guess your name is Barstow, ain't it? You seem pretty handy givin' advice."

The big man's cheeks showed a faint surprise, like an elephant might if a mouse stepped on him. His eyes came back to Andros' face and a pale glint touched his arrogant stare.

35

"Certainly I'm Barstow."

His lambent glance raked Andros' garb and an amused grin tugged the corners of his mouth. "Who'd you think—"

"Mr. Barstow," the girl said hurriedly, "owns the Half-Circle Arrow—"

"Which bestows on him, I reckon, a God-given right to jerk the plums from his neighbors' pies."

Saying which, Andros' left hand fished the makings from a pocket of his shirt. The same hand smoothly rolled his smoke and his tongue licked a wet line across its flap while his stare lashed color to the big man's cheeks. "I've met a lot of Barstows in my time. None of 'em ever amounted to much."

He let that lay while he got a match from his hatband, briskly raked it across his chaps. He said around his cigarette: "I don't expect this guy will, either."

Barstow's lip corners lost their smile. Quick-flaring anger changed the set of his cheeks and his lifting fists were bunching when he suddenly shrugged. A wry grin crooked his heavy mouth. He said, "You're probably right," and turned to the girl, ignoring Andros.

"About that matter we were discussing yesterday . . . Expect you've made your mind up—"

The slow and negative move of her head stopped his talk in mid-sentence. "No," she said, and two small lines showed across her forehead. "No." There was a quick appeal in the look she gave him. "Reb, I've got to have more time—"

"Time!" A scowl cut an angular path through the twist of his cheeks. Compressed lips showed the run of his thoughts. He swung broad shoulders roughly, yet checked the gesture with a savage impulse and darkly eyed the open palms of his beefy hands. He rubbed those palms across the coarse blue weave of his trousers with a slow and circling motion while his frowning stare traced the carpet's pattern. He brought his head up restlessly. A quick half-turn shoved his big hands deep and brusquely into the pockets of his coat. They bunched there, knuckles showing plainly against the bulged-out fabric.

The things that were in his mind abruptly got the best of him. "By God," he growled vehemently, "you know the way to keep a man afire! I don't *want* to be held off! I want my answer now!"

"Don't press me, Reb." There was a softness and a pleading

in the timbre of Flame's voice. "Don't insist on having your answer tonight. Let me have more time, Reb—"

"*Time?* Does it take a woman forty-eight hours to make up her mind if she wants a man?"

She stood there with her lips apart, her quickened breathing lifting her breasts, her eyes upon him gravely, appearing to study the half-crouched shadow his shape threw against the wall. His large, cream-colored Stetson was shoved far back from his forehead showing the rebellious tangle of his thick and sandy hair.

"It sometimes takes a great deal longer, Reb," she answered quietly. "Love doesn't always come like the crack of a pistol; quite often it is a slow, steady-growing process, careful to find its true measure in a man's real worth. It's not just a question of whether I want you or not—you know that. There are other things to consider. Things I've got to get clear in my mind."

Barstow scowled at her, saying nothing, roan cheeks showing the sultry turbulence of his thoughts.

"After all, Reb," she said reflectively, "we've know each other a pretty long while. Until just recently we've not found the need to speak of—"

"When I make up my mind to a thing, I *want* it!" he said loudly. "I want *you!*" An' I want you *now!* By God I don't propose to stand twiddlin' my thumbs—"

She said: "Reb!" and waited till, with the anger plain on his cheeks, he stopped. "Where is the need of all this rush? Why must I give you my answer now? Why won't tomorrow do just as well?—or next week? If I loved you now, don't you think I'd love you as much tomorrow or the next day?"

He looked at her, a film of caution slowly crowding the anger out of his glance. But his cheeks still showed the sullenness of him and arrogance was a white-rimmed line in the surly twist of his lips. Her spunk seeemd at once to anger him and to please him. Yet resentment was the greatest force bottled in him at the moment. Few persons had had the temerity to balk his known designs.

"You know how it is with me," he muttered, coming as near an apology as his nature could ever let him. "It ain't that I've any doubt of you—it's just that I ain't no hand for waitin'. Never had to," he added belligerently. "I always been

37

strong for doing things right now. Bred to it—my ol' man was hell for settling things in a hurry."

A thought kicked over with suden clarity in Andros' mind. The look he fixed on Barstow showed a keen and close attention. He did not speak; but a risen interest was apparent in the hunching of his shoulders.

Neither of the principals noticed him. The girl said, "Yes, I know. You've told me that before. But it happens I'm just not built that way, Reb. You'll have to wait until—"

"*Wait!*" Barstow ground the word out, the anger in him heating up. "I've waited too long already. I'll have my answer *now* by God!"

He said it flatly and his face took on a harsher cast, his ruddy skin showing heightened color. He was palpably a prideful man and one who had got his own way too long to care anything for the wants of others. This girl's stubbornness was a thing to be crushed; she must learn he was master of all he surveyed. His eyes said so plainly. It was in the harsh snarl of his words.

"No Barstow ever begged for a woman's favors. I'm takin' my answer! Yes or no?"

Andros bent his head and went out the door. His spurs, dragging over the planking, etched jingling sound in the silence behind. He gathered up his pony's reins and struck out for the black outline of a yonder stable. Abruptly he stopped and came wheeling round. He retraced his way to the hitchrail. He paused by Barstow's horse and put a swift hand across its flanks. He looked at the hand with lips curling. Afterwards he turned and went back to the stable.

The night was now black and thick as velvet and the soundings of nocturnal insects were like tiny flutes in the stillness. He tramped along, grim locked in his thoughts, quick mind stabbing questions at this discovery he had made about Barstow. He gave no attention to where his boots took him; he went plowing along with all his accustomed care relaxed.

He reached the stable and, still intent on his problem, went tramping inside and peeled the gear from his horse. With the same abstraction he rubbed the animal down and put an ample measure of grain within its reach. Then he quit the place and headed for the bunkhouse.

That building's lamp flung oblong patches of yellow brilliance into this enfolding darkness, relieving it somewhat in the immediate vicinity and elsewhere made a vagueness of the night-black shadows. Against these light lanes Andros made out the silhouetted shapes of loitering men. He saw enough to understand their eyes were focused on him. These, he guessed, must be the punchers Flame had mentioned. They were men who would judge another by the things that other did within their sight. Experience with their kind had taught Clem Andros that peculiar wisdom.

He wheeled his shoulders toward them, swift to cross lamp's brightness where it spilled from the open doorway. A streak of flame bit instantly toward him from the yonder gloom. Cat-quick he whirled his lean shape slanchways as a pistol's clamor stilled the insects' chorus. One blurred flip spun his gun to hand. He drove his lead through the slatted outline of the corral's peeled poles and straightened as a stifled cry sheared through the dimming echoes.

Against those denser shadows by the corral gate a dark shape tipped forward, supported by the outflung arm that gripped a corral bar. Andros, striding forward, held his fire, but his spurs clanked harshly as he crossed the yard.

When there were but ten paces between himself and that bent shape he stopped. "You cut your string a little close that time, friend."

Cranston's jaw was clenched. His teeth shone palely between parted lips and his eyes were bitter with the fury of his balked intention. He said: "By God—" and fell with Andros' bullet in his chest.

6

LONG ROPE

THE SCREEN door banged at the ranch house. Barstow's shape came plowing through the gloom, came stamping from the shadows, striding savagely toward the crumpled figure by the gate. Someone else came, too, stopping a little way behind. Andros' shoulders impatiently stirred, and he wheeled his torso half around to send a raking look across that halted person.

It was Flame Tarnell. She had no hat and her hair was tumbled by the wind. Her look was on him with a strained attention. Her breasts showed disturbed by a quickened breathing and she had one hand upflung before them as though to fend off something ugly. "Who *are* you?" Her whispered words were choked with feeling.

He had his moment of hesitation then. He guessed the expression of her face would be in his head forever. But he could not regret having killed the saddle tramp, Cranston; the man had made his play and Andros had called it. It was that simple. Life or death. You had your choice.

He slid his pistol back in leather and twisted his shoulders to where his glance might follow Barstow's moving shape. He watched the big man pause by Cranston's booted feet and stand there, stilled by a rigid interest. His soft-snarled oath reached Andros plainly; and then he was turning striding across the yard again, his big shape swinging a grotesque shadow, his flat roan cheeks inscrutably set.

Andros had no need to guess what answer Flame had given this fellow. The revelation of her decision was in the sullen cast of all his features, it was in the traveling swing of him, in the jerk and leap of his muscles.

Andros caught Flame's lifted voice again. She stepped from the murk beside him, one white hand reaching out to fall upon his sleeve and instantly stop him. "Who are you?" she repeated. He read wonder in that quick-breathed phrase; wonder and anxiety, and a something else that stirred his pulses oddly.

Her upturned face was ashine in the lamp's refracted glow. He stared long at her and the leaping blood slogged through him with tremendous acceleration. It was a vivid, compelling moment that got beneath his guard, stirring up long-dead emotions, jarring him loose of that cold implacability with which he had gunned Cranston. He had no thought of Cranstone now. He almost forgot Reb Barstow.

But not for long.

Barstow's heavy tones growled: "Yes! It's time we had a handle to you!"

Andros turned. The move was entirely unhurried. Every enquiring line of his face was coolly tranquil. "Getting nervous?"

"Nervous?" Reb Barstow scowled. "It'll take more'n any dead saddle bum to make *me* nervous, bucko. I don't like

40

havin' strangers round—particularly the gun-packin' kind that don't dare let their names out."

"I'm not scared of my name. Andros is what I'm called; Clem Andros. Sometimes known as *Black*."

Something bleak and frantic rushed the rancher's whitened cheeks and was instantly blanked by a lifted, watchful vigilance.

But Andros had seen. Sardonically his glance reached out to Flame Tarnell. But her expression had not changed. "Black Andros" was just a name to her, just an ordinary name without any connotation. Relief bathed Andros in a blessed wave—until he caught the thin-lipped smile that was twisting the rancher's features.

"I'd best have the boys unfurl the flag. This is quite an occasion, bucko. Ain't every spread can boast entertainin' the *king of gunslicks*."

Andros' smile matched Barstow's own. "I don't think yours'll be able to. Generally I aim to steer plumb clear of rattlers' nests an' polecat burrows."

Barstow's cheeks surged bright with color. His smile peeled thin and an ugly glitter crept into the stare from his down-squeezed eyelids. "I don't like that—"

"I guess you know what to do then." Andros grinned at him, teeth coldly bared in the moonlight.

Barstow's shape whipped clear around. "You get rid of this fellow, Flame, right now! Get him outa here! He's nothin' but a stinkin' *Texas man!* Havin' him round'll be just shoutin' for trouble—"

"*Who's* trouble?" Andros chuckled.

Flame said, "You'd better be going now, Reb. You've quite a ride and it's getting late. When I want advice—"

Barstow snarled, "You'll want it, all right! An' *need* it!"

"Then," Flame told him with lifted chin, "I expect I can find it closer to home. Goodnight, Reb."

Barstow gave her one long dark look and went storming off, the clank of his spur rowels harsh as a jay's call, the twist of his features a pale mask of hate.

Flame said to Andros abruptly, "I'll see you in the morning. Goodnight."

Andros put no trust in the bunkhouse, nor in the sloe-eyed punchers who so silently had planted Cranston. He carried

41

his blankets into the felted gloom of the pink-barked pines and squatted long moments there on his bootheels, watching the moon through the sighing limbs, before at last he crawled into them.

He was up before the sun crossed the peaks and swam for a cold five minutes in the icy waters of a gurgling creek that fed the eighty-foot tank in the yard. Then he climbed back into his wrinkled black garb and buckled the scuffed black chaps on over his dark-checked trousers. He buckled on his gun belt, too, and carefully inspected the big, sheathed pistols that sagged its greasy holsters before he started for the mess shack where cook's triangle was banging the call to chuck.

He entered the shack prepared for anything, well knowing his knack for making enemies and alive to the likelihood that there might be one man here who drew some portion of his pay from Barstow. There was last night's shooting to be considered, also; Cranston may not have been a popular man, but he'd been their boss—it might add up to something.

If it did he found no betrayal in the schooled looks of these punchers. They were all here. Three of them were eating and the other, an older man, was busy with the steaming pots on the stove top. There was a dogged method in the way these men kept shoveling the food to their faces. They maintained an adopted silence and kept their eyes on their plates. He was made to feel his place as an outlander; and by their manner these men showed what welcome they extended. He could, Andros mused morosely, have put it on his eyeball and never felt the pain.

But he was hungry. He attacked his food with vigor. The same old fare—plain beans and bacon and sourdough biscuits washed down with hot black coffee. But it tasted good to Clem Andros with his feet beneath a table.

He had his meal half finished and the punchers, shoving back their chairs, were getting out the makings when Flame Tarnell came in through the open doorway and stopped in the lamplight's pale effulgence to call a brief goodmorning.

The punchers grunted, nodding their heads, and got promptly busy with tobacco and papers. The girl showed the strain of a sleepless night. She raised one arm toward Clem Andros. "This is Andros, boys—the new range boss." Her look pointed out each in turn to him: "Curly, Pecos Jim, Tom Flaurity, Coldfoot Dan."

The men looked up at him briefly and went on rolling their quirlies. They neither spoke nor nodded. Nor did Andros acknowledge their acquaintance. He went hard on with his eating. He had sized these fellows up when he came in and their names added nothing new to the score.

They were a typical crew; lean-hipped, bold fellows with the mark of the saddle on them and the marks of the sun and wind. Their like could be found on forty outfits in this wild Arizona country. An average group. One thing stamped them for what they were—the bold, dark look of their faces. The basic difference that sets the range man apart from his fellows is that individual liberty, that lawlessness that a wild land inculcates in a man, that tough adherence to his own set notions and standards, that scorn of all other conceptions. He is impatient of rules and enforced restraint; he makes his own code and abides by it.

The men tramped out when their smokes were finished.

Andros concluded his breakfast and sat ruminatively smoking himself while he waited for Flame Tarnell to get finished with hers. He felt no particular jubilation or pride as a result of Flame's proclamation.

He did feel a little curious though to know what had changed her mind. He had his own suspicion; but mostly he was concerned with how his job as foreman here might effect his agreement with Bocart. It might make its fulfillment either more difficult or easy according to what pattern events might take. But he knew one small satisfaction; this job of ramrod for the Rocking T gave him reason for remaining in this Four Peaks country.

Last night he'd found it good to be in this girl's company; it had seemed in some measure completeness. This morning his mood was different. He got no ease from her presence. She was too vivid a personality, too personal a factor. There was dynamite in her, disturbing to the accustomed run of a man's cool thinking.

Putting down her fork she shoved her chair a little way back from the table and turned her head to look at him. "You have my thanks," she said, "for what you did in town last night. In payment of that score I've put you in as foreman here. You wanted that job and you have it. Understand though, I'm not condoning that affair with Crans—"

"What I did for Cranston has nothing to do with your affairs."

"Oh!" Her eyes showed suddenly angry. There was deeper color in the curve of her cheeks. "Then let's have it understood right now you're not to pack private quarrels here—"

"I didn't pack it here—"

"Must we bandy words? You deliberately killed the man you call Cranston!"

"Yes, ma'am. I reckon I did. I most usually figure to kill a snake when I find one—particularly one that tries to bite me. I'm makin' no apologies for it."

Flame's quick stare was sharp and cold. She had lived too long in the West to be shocked by Andros' blunt words or by the code that prompted them. But she was angry—mighty angry, Andros thought; and something else was there in her stare. Scorn, perhaps. He had no time to convince himself, for just then Flame said bitterly: "So you're what Reb Barstow said you were—what he called you to your face! A hired-gun hombre!"

Andros shrugged. He made no remark. If she chose to think that, let her. Might be best all round—certainly best for her. There was no place for a woman in the life of Black Clem Andros. He felt no regret for having killed Cranston. The man was a plain damn horse thief; Andros knew this of experience, and that same experience had proved the man a double crosser as well. Five sheriffs were hunting Cranston's scalp. The country was well rid of him.

Flame said abruptly, gravely: "I had too much to think about to do any sleeping last night. Talmage Vargas—you had better know this—will be bringing his sheep back through here again. He's due most any time now. It's going to mean the end of the Four Peaks cow business . . . if he's permitted to get away with it."

But she was fair. "That's putting it pretty much up to you—"

"That's all right—"

"But it isn't—not really. It's not your fight; it's not your land or your country."

"I like this country," Andros said. "It's got room for a man to stretch himself—"

"Not any more, I'm afraid. It used to be like that. But now it's just got room for one thing—sheep."

44

Her stare met Andros' straightly. "I've changed my mind. You can't be my foreman. I've got no right—"

"Shucks," Andros said, "don't waste your breath. It's up to you whether I boss this spread, but wild horses couldn't drag me out of this country now." He paraded his tough-hombre smile for her. "Why, ma'am, this thing comin' up is just what hired 'guns comb the border for. You'd better have me with you than teamed up with someone against you."

Her indrawn breath made a quick, sharp sound. She sat stiff as if he'd struck her. "You—"

"Go on," he said, "let's hear the rest."

Her glance stayed on him a moment longer; bright, ice cold, disdainful. Then it wheeled away. She said a trifle stiffly, "There isn't any rest."

"Of course there is. There always is in things like this. Vargas had you on the hip last time. You had some cattle left, didn't you? All right; that's why he beat you. You had property you were scared of losing. Kept you on the defensive, didn't it?"

Her glance came back with an odd, searching thoughtfulness. "Yes."

"But you've lost your cattle now," he said. "The drought an' sheep have ruined you. What steers you got left wouldn't bring a dollar a hoof at the glue factory. They're nothin' but hide an' bone. I've seen 'em. So now you can roll up your sleeves an' give Vargas your full attention. Can't you?"

"I can't do much by myself—"

"You can *try*."

Andros rolled up another smoke while he left her to think it over. "Nothin's so bad as you think it is. These Four Peaks ranchers need organizing; they've got to be talked into fighting Talmage Vargas solid. No single one of you could do a thing against him. You've got to trot out some teamwork. You've got to fight him together—all for one and one for all."

"You make it sound very convincing—"

"It's a cinch," Andros said. "All you need is a leader."

"Yes. That's all." She pushed the hair back out of her eyes. "We found that out when the sheep came last time." She stopped then, stared at her booted feet for a moment. Then her eyes came swiftly up and she said: "You're sure you want to do this?"

Andros chuckled. "I wouldn't be here if I didn't."

45

"Very well," Flame said. She swung from her chair and paced the room. "If you lick the sheep you can have half this ranch—"

"I'm doin' this 'cause I want to—"

She faced him with her throat a tight line. "You'll fight on *my* terms or not at all."

"Okey," Andros said picking up his hat. "Many thanks for the grub—"

"Where you going?"

"That depends. Comin' down off your high horse?"

Her brown eyes stared at him very bright. "I think I hate you, Andros."

"That's all right. A lot of folks do." There was little humor in Andros' grin. "I never play the other man's game. I call the turn where I hire my guns. An' there'll be a couple strings to it, too. Have you got your mind made up yet? About what you'll do if the sheep come?"

"If the sheep come back I'll fight," she said.

It was Andros now who threw cold water. "With what?"

"With the last gasp of life left in me!" She meant it, too.

Looking into her eyes he could not doubt it. He considered her with a probing interest. "You know how long you'd last agaist Vargas?"

"That's one of the reasons I'm hiring you."

He let that pass. "Can you trust these punchers?" He ignored the cook's look. "Would you trust them like you would a brother?"

"I—" She hesitated, then said with her chin up: "Certainly."

"And what about these other small outfits? Think they'll throw in with you?" He rested one hip on the table.

She looked doubtful. But she said, "They might."

"Which ones?"

She stared at the cupboard; stood considering. "Flowerpot would—I'd bet on them. And Spur and the Boxed Q—they'd help, too." She bit her lip and a frown showed how desperately she tried to convince herself there were others. She said, "I think Lazy J and Tadpole might come in if we talked fast and the chances didn't look too terrible against us. But that's all, I guess. There's others, but I'm afraid they'll do their cheering from the sidelines."

"Or," Andros said with his cynical smile, "they might *not* cheer at all. Ain't that it?"

Her nod was reluctant. "I'm afraid so."

46

"Those spreads you named—how many men could we count on from them?"

"Sixteen, perhaps. Not more."

"Say twenty, counting yours."

Andros got to his feet, crushing his cigarette out on his plate. "I'll see what I can do," he said. "But make no mistake. I'll have to have full rein here. No half-way stuff will cut it."

He watched her grimly, wrinkles cracking the hat-paled smoothness of his forehead. "We've got to have this plain right now. When I make out to run something, I aim to run it—all the way. Is that clear? I'll not be hounded with questions. I'll not be stopped with recriminations. I'll do whatever I have to do an' you'll have to trust my judgment. There'll be times when you're not going to like it."

Once more her nod came. Slowly. "I guess I can stand it." She gave him a moment's probing scrutiny then, but whatever her thoughts he could not read them. He had his wistful moment, seeing what this girl could mean to a man big enough to win her—to Barstow, maybe, if at some later time they patched their quarrel. He tried not to scowl as he thought of that.

Sun's glow lay warm along her cheeks and the sheen of her hair was a midnight black. The nearness, the desirability and the vivid fullness of her grabbed and pummeled him, tore beneath his guard and turned him harshly savage.

The cook went out and Andros took a half step toward her, then pulled up suddenly with the knuckles of his clenched fists white as far-North snow.

He said roughly, "I better get along," and wheeled out past her, ducking his head as he went through the door.

The idling punchers were by the corral. Three of them appeared busily whittling; a task they continued. But the fourth, a redhead, looked up coldly as Andros stopped.

Andros said, "If a man was figurin' to air his views before a choice assortment of this country's neighbors, where'd he do his talkin' if he didn't want the sheep crowd hearin' it?"

"Flowerpot," Coldfoot murmured. He kept on whittling.

"All right; I want Boxed Q, Lazy J an' Tadpole notified immediate that Rocking T is holdin' a powwow there tomorrow night. Scatter."

A couple of the boys half-heartedly picked up their ropes. But the gaunt, rehaired Tom Flaurity kept his place on the opera seat. He looked down at Andros stolidly, shifted his quid and spat. "Them Miz' Tarnell's orders?"

"They're *my* orders," Andros said, and yanked him off his perch. "You git in a saddle pronto."

It was noon with a hot sun smashing fury when Andros rode alertly into Long Rope's daytime somnolence. Its single street lay stark in the sunlight, playground of dust and fluttering rubbish. There was no animation on it save for the flight of an occasional paper and the restive shifting of the six tethered ponies racked at the shadeless hitchrail fronting the big saloon. He tied his own bronc there with the feel of malignant eyes upon him. With stiff-held head he stepped upon the scorching walk, and off it onto the saloon veranda, as deserted now as the street it flanked.

With a quick sideways move he was through the slatted doors and sweeping one raking glance the length of the dim, near-empty room. A shirtsleeved man whose pear-shaped middle was hid behind a dirty apron was behind the bar spelling out the text of a week-old paper. Two men in range clothes midway down one tabled side sat with their heads above a bottle. There was no one else in sight.

Andros crossed the sawdust sprinkled floor and stopped with an elbow on the bar beside the reader's paper. The barman's glance came up and abruptly widened. The end of a pink tongue crossed his lips. "My Gawd," he murmured, *"Andros!"*

A cold amusement briefly laid its glint across Andros' glance.

"Morning, Turly. I'll take two fingers of the best," he said; and wondered at the strong uneasiness of the barman's manner. He had casually known this man five years ago when Turly had run a gambling dive at Ogden. There'd been no particular enmity between them; nothing to account for this queer unease that so markedly was bothering Turly now.

Then he caught a blur of movement in the back bar mirror; a woman's face coming swiftly toward him—a face he remembered with quickening pulses.

Her lips were red in the back bar's mirror and curved in a look of pleased surprise. He saw in her eyes things he'd rather were not there; saw the touch of warm color that brushed her cheeks. It was the girl in whose behalf he had antagonized Joce Latham in the San Carlos hashhouse.

48

Plainly she remembered him. With tightening lips Andros turned to face her.

"Oh!" she said. "So it's really you! I'm glad! I—" she stopped; and all the light and eagernes fell completely from her features, leaving them twisted and haggard with startled fear. Andros' stabbing glance caught the face of Barstow hugely grinning from a window that opened out onto the veranda. He heard in that instant the opening creak of the batwing doors.

He stood with all his muscles screaming and thought how his fate ever followed patterns; how each thing at its appointed time dropped snugly in place to mock and trap him.

With a sideways leap he flung his torso clear around. Stillness stretched like a wire in this place. Joce Latham was coming in on the balls of his feet with one white clamped fist tightly gripping a gun stock.

7

"YOU'RE NOT A CLEVER LIAR, BISHOP—"

ANDROS stood beside the girl and watched cool reason crawl away. He stood with brown fists dangling empty and knew it had to be this way. He could not explain this girl to Latham. Blood would tell—blood and the things in a man's hot head. Desire for revenge was a still white flame in the gambler's stare.

"So you *did* come after all," Latham purred. "I thought you would—you wench stealin' rat!" Turbulent fires were aboil inside him, searing away the ropes of his caution, driving their robust fury storm-black across the scowling twist of his face. San Carlos was in his rage-fogged mind and this white-cheeked girl was in it too; and a pulse on his forehead was throbbing wildly. *"I'll fix you!"* he shouted, and fired point-blank.

But rage's red flare played hell with his aim. Andros, braced, took the impact of that shot without leaving his tracks. He seemed to lean a little forward as though he might be welcoming it. All saw the dust jump out of his vest.

He straightened slowly.

"You fool!" he said; and flame was a white streak that jumped from the pistol some unseen magic had conjured to his hand. Latham's eyes sprang wide in shocked unbelief. Wind off the hill-slopes crossed the room, swirling the stringers of blue smoke round them. The girl was like a statue—tranced. The men beyond hung tense by their table, their startled looks gone stiff and frozen. A shudder ran through him and Latham dropped. Like a tall, sleek aspen to the bite of steel.

Time stretched and thinned. Andros stood immobile, hunched shoulders set, his vacuous stare seeing all before him while the big gun gaped its menace from his hand. He watched, for this was a care ground into him by all those years of turbulence Krell's death had made a mockery. It was a care he could not put away though weariness tugged every nerve and muscle and that pain in his side was a sharp, barbed blade some devil was twisting, twisting, twisting.

First to break the tableau, he moved at last and turned his head toward that window where Reb Barstow had stood and grinned at him. Barstow still was framed in it but his grin had gone twisted—ludicrous. Gone was all of his displayed enjoyment. The heavy slant of his stiff roan cheeks obscured his thought; but changed ideas, a new perception, had thrust haunted shadows beneath his eyes.

A last flare of anger had its way with Andros. Barstow had known Joce Latham was coming—had probably egged him on. That was Barstow's craft. Andros' stare was brightly wicked. "You wantin' to pack this on from where Joce dropped it?"

Oddly, Barstow displayed no anger. He stood coldly still and shook his head. In the roan of his cheeks was a strange perplexity. His amber eyes held lifted caution. He had the look of a man uncertain, a man slow groping toward an unwanted conclusion.

His shoulders stirred with abrupt impatience. "Not me, bucko. I can wait for mine," he said, and wheeled from the window, the stamp of his boots growing fainter and fainter.

One moment longer Andros watched the window. Then his glance came round, raking the look of those men by the table —searching the still white mobile face of that one lone girl who stood so stiff in this room's frozen quiet.

A curious numbness crawled over Andros. His will would

not function; his sight was grown hazy. He could not understand why the place was so cold, or his veins were like fire, or his pistol so heavy. The pain of his side was grown monstrous, ugly.

He became suddenly aware that the girl was moving. She was coming toward him. Her eyes were funny and her features twisted with a plain emotion he could not account for. Anxiety—yes! That was it—anxiety. Perhaps, after all, she had really loved Latham. But no! Anxiety was for the living; the dead were beyond it—and she was looking at *him*. He could not understand it. She had one hand hard against her breasts; the other stretched toward him—a queer, unfathomable gesture.

Ed Turly's voice came strictly grave. "The king is dead. Long live the king."

Crazy thing to say!

Andros, with his straining gaze on the men by the table, said: "Turly! Come out from behind that bar where I can see you!"

He heard Turly moving.

The light was bad, was failing rapidly. It was a haze, like smoke, all run together. The men by the table were vague-placed shapes, uncertain as ghosts in this ghastly gloom.

In the vaulted quiet he could hear the shuffle of Turly's feet as the barman came from behind the mahogany. He saw the gray mass of Turly's soiled apron move against the white wall.

He wondered angrily why Turly did not light the lamps.

He swept a glance at the girl and shook his head from side to side. But it did not help. Her face was a blob, one pale smear against this gloom. It seemed to be floating. Her legs— Why, she hadn't any legs! Her face, in the haze, kept swimming closer.

He put one hand before him to stop it, to fend it off "That's far enough, ma'am. Just stop right there." He brought the muzzle of his sixgun up; or he meant to. But someway his hand was like lead. It was heavy and numb and he could not move it.

And that cursed fire in his veins—it was burning him up. His lips were stiff, they felt cracked and feverish. His tongue wouldn't move.

He peered toward the men he had seen by the table. Two

51

dark lumps that seemed curiously bent forward as though they were about to fall over.

He commanded his wabbly legs to move and was childishly pleased when he found they obeyed him. Still watching the lumps by the table he backed to the bar. Still facing the room he hooked his elbows over it. He hung there that way with his knees all turned to water. With a straining care he watched the two lumps that had once been men beside a table.

Outside a wagon or something went by and filled this big room with its clatter and rattling and the smell of its dust got into his nostrils.

He wondered why no one had come to find out about those shots he'd fired. No—he'd only fired once. That was right. Latham had fired an then he had fired. Two shots in all. In this dead town that should have been aplenty to bring men running. Maybe they'd moved; gone away to some better place. That kind of tickled him. He thought they'd not have to look very far to find one.

Damn the light anyway. It was so dark now he could not see the rear of this place. He could not see the lumps any longer, or Turly's apron. Even that girl—he could hear her breathing—was but a vague silhouetted shadow.

As from miles away Turly's voice came dimly. "Don't you reckon, Clem, it's gettin' time we racked the chips?"

Andros' mind could not shape an answer. A strange weird peace was stealing over him. He felt quaintly drowsy as though he'd been sitting too long in the sun. It was only by the sheerest effort he kept his eyes from closing and his sagging chin from hitting his chest. It took a world of effort.

His thoughts became disjointed and held no bearing on the thing in hand. They took him back along the trail to things he'd done in other times. And then he had no thoughts at all and everything about him was a solid black and he found the peace he sought.

The Upland road that, going by Barstow's, led to the country beyond Diamond Mountain, crossed Rocking T range within mocking bird's call of the Tarnell ranch house. A hoof-stamped trail that strangely twisted, following meticulously in its dips and windings the lazy meanderings of the curling creek.

Flame Tarnell had watched that road since five o'clock

this evening. It was nine and the moon would be soon coming up now; and Clem Andros had not returned.

Flame Tarnell was restless, and she was not a restless girl. A vague uneasiness had crept upon her and she could not cast it off. She told herself again, more firmly, that her range boss' absence had no least part in it; but intuition said she lied. She turned from the window and crossed the room aimlessly, and there wheeled and came back without lighting the lamp. Yes; she admitted it; Clem Andros' nonappearance *did* have considerable to do with her strange uneasiness.

She was filled with a bleak foreboding.

There were men abroad in the dark of this night. Furtive riders. Dark shapes crouched with their hats pulled low, with chests down-bent above their saddles. This was a little used trail of late, and yet she'd counted six men riding north since dusk.

Abruptly she backed with a quick catch of breath. There a seventh man went, right now, slipping by without sound in the curdled shadows!

She caught her lip between her teeth and crouched there with a pounding heart. This stealthy traffic held implications. There was something sinister in those vague-seen shapes.

Flame was twenty-two and all her life had lived in this hard land: had lived and watched and learned, to some extent, to gauge this country's moods. Intangible stealth flowed darkly through this silent night, and the vagrant wind soughing through the pine tops was dreary and dismal. A soul in anguish.

There was light in the bunkhouse, low turned and dim.

Straightening presently she pulled up a chair and sat down by the window where her anxious eyes could continue their vigil. She was acting like an idiot, and told herself so, tartly. It did not help much. She thought of Andros.

She had thought about him many times. He was the kind of man she'd dreamed of in the loneliness of this wild solitude. He was some way different, unlike other men she'd known. He was capable; efficiency was in his every gesture. Yet he had a quietness and deference which she had secretly found attractive. She liked to listen to the soft Texas drawl of his talk, to watch the clean white flash of his teeth behind the lazy smile that sometimes briefly curved his lips. His arrival, she thought, had changed things somehow; had shifted values

53

and given her the first real sense of security she had known since her father's death.

She stood up and, crossing to the table, lit the lamp. She drew on her riding gauntlets and paused a bit uncertainly beside the table, finally to pull off the gloves and toss them indifferently on the lounge. She turned then, hesitantly, and paused, surveying the sleek and emptly blackness of the window on which were superimposed reflected portions of the room behind her.

She shrugged, turned away with affected nonchalance and strolled aimlessly about examining various trophies hung upon the walls, the oak-framed Remingtons, the Navajo blankets, that Mexican sombrero with its silver threads and tiny bells and band of gleaming conchos.

She went to the fireplace, her eyes on the border rifles crossed above it. She wondered idly if perhaps a little fire might not improve her spirits. She did not build one though. Her glance roved across the mantel, came to thoughtful rest upon the deep-seamed features of that tough and gaunt old man in the beaten silver frame.

Her eyes grew soft and wistful and she forgot for a moment the most of her fears. She smiled at the pictured face determinedly. She must show him she was not afraid. She *wasn't* afraid. A little moody maybe—daunsy, as the cowboys said; but not afraid. She put the thought into words. "If the sheep come again I'll fight, Dad. It's been rough round here, but there's a man on the spread that'll back me now. He six feet tall; he's slim and sometimes he's handsome. But mostly he's got an odd, tight look—like you used to have when things got to crowding. I wish you could meet him, Dad. You'd like him. . . . Things are going to be different now with him around."

A floorboard creaked and she whirled with paling cheeks. But no intruder was crouched behind her. There was no one in the room but herself. She thought: "Just the old house settling," and laughed a little, flustered.

She went back and paused by the window. She pressed her face against it, with her hands cupped by her cheeks, and saw three men come out of the bunkhouse. They squatted down in the moonglow with their backs to the bunkhouse wall. She watched them dig out the inevitable makings. She could not hear what they talked about, but moments later she thought to raise the window a mite and she found they were talking of horses.

She felt soothed some way, quieted by these familiar things. She pulled her chair to the table; picked up and opened a book. But in this mood no printed page could hold her; the masterful figure and dark commanding features of the range boss kept coming between it and herself.

She wondered where he was tonight. He had gone, she thought, to town. He had not taken her into his confidence. Well . . . that was the bargain. No questions.

Strong interest and her feminine pique of riddle drove her into speculation concerning other things about him, just as it had a thousand times since his coming. Where was he from? Who was he? She had sensed on more than one occasion the deep streak of bitterness that was in him. It excited her curiosity. What thing from a hidden past still held the power to torture him? What had he done that was so grave that even now it must color his actions? Or was it something that another had done . . .? Who *was* he? Who *was* Black Clem Andros? That he was a man of import was definitely proved. She had seen Reb Barstow's face when he heard that name.

Andros was cool, quick-thinking, dangerous. She had been around men long enough to know. Her mind went back to the look in his eye when, tapping Grave Creek Charlie's shoulder, he'd taken up the sheepman's challenge; to that darkly tranquil slanting of his cheeks when last night Barstow in this room had likened him to Cranston; to the saturnine curling of Andros' lips when to Barstow's face he'd disparaged the Barstow tribe. Yes, the man was dangerous; the cut of his mouth and the slant of his jaw were certainly not those of a pacifist.

She recalled other things about him. The softness of his step. The sure quick way of his shoulders. The steadfast directness of his gaze. Queer how great a claim he'd made upon her thoughts.

She remembered him as he'd looked in town the night she had first seen him—could it really have been but last night? A black-haired man with dark, burnt skin pulled toughly across high cheekbones; a man whose eyes were the color of smoky sage. She could see, as though he stood right now before her, the grim lips cleaving that wind-whipped face above his cold and saturnine jaw. She saw with an awakened clarity how that battered hat shoved back from his bony forehead clearly typified her whole impression of him. A thing of service, unostentatious and uncared for, it yet displayed with an odd completeness the brash and mocking confidence of the man.

He was tall, lean, sure. He had a physical toughness that characterized each tiniest shred of gesture; not a blatant swaggerer's toughness, yet nonetheless impossible of concealment. He was one who stood full head and shoulders above the level of his fellows, a man who had heard the owl hoot. A vital, colorful figure.

And so Flame sat and mused. Not the display of animal brawn, but the sturdy character to be read in Andros' features it was that so swiftly had captured the girl's imagination. Those features told of experience beyond his years; they told that well, but they told more—in them crouched strong hint of their owner's staunch, unswervable viewpoint, the adamantine quality of purpose that would send Black Andros clear through hell before he'd lay aside or be balked out of completing any chore he'd put his hand to. This trait shone like a thread of silver through the cynical mockery of the look with which he viewed his enemies.

He made a long, efficient shape in his scarred black chaps and flannel rider's shirt. His confidence was like an impregnable rock; yet, combined and toned with that quiet deference he showed her, this very quality, she felt sure, must be the uncarriable barrier against which all her troubles would beat in vain.

The thought was tremendously reassuring.

But Andros was no man of iron; she knew him to be very human, as prone to likes and dislikes as any other. He had his prejudices—strong ones, sudden ones; they were plain in the swift impatient stirring of his shoulders. She had marked that habit more than once.

Moreover, he was a man who made mistakes, and had made others in the past. Could one forget or ever miss the caustic bitterness which was so much a part of him? And the rash, quick-striking temper of him that could lift like a flare of light!

These were his weaknesses and—

Her reflections and evaluations of Clem Andros were suddently scattered by the whooming, hollow boom of horses'

56

hoofs across the bridge. With one hand caught up to her throat she straightened tensely, throbbing premonitorily to the rush of yonder horsemen and their stop before the bunkhouse.

A definite alarm took her hurrying to the window. She crouched with face pressed against it, recognition of those riders touching her instantly. They were men from the Half-Circle Arrow; Barstow's foreman, Bishop Torril, and one other—Bronc Culebra. Excitement ran their lifted voices; her men showed an avid interest. Fragments of that talk came to her, swinging her round with whitened cheeks and pushing her throught the outside door.

"Got 'im, all right, I say. Plugged 'im—"

"Yeah. He shore looked like the wrath of Gawd with them elbows hooked to the bar that way an' them damn eyes of his a-borin' holes through me an' Bronc, here, over the muzzle of that hawglaig!"

"Downed 'im, eh?" That was Flaurity's voice, with satisfaction—the last Flame heard as she pulled the door shut after her. The stiff night wind shoved against her face, roughing her hair and whipping her skirt out gustily as she made for the dark group by the bunkhouse.

She came hurrying up unnoticed just as Torril said, "An' served him plumb right, if you're askin' me—the goddam meddler "

Flame caught at Torril's stirrup; cried breathlessly, "What is it, Bishop? Are you talking about my range boss—about Clem Andros? Oh! what *is* it? What has *happened?*"

Culebra shifted his chaw and spat. Bishop Torril said, "Ain't nothin' to get up a lather over." And Culebra leered at her wickedly.

Tom Flaurity got up and came over to her, taking off his wide-rimmed hat. "Now, Miz' Flame, ma'am," he said soothingly, "this yere ain't nothin' fer you t' bother yore purty haid about. You jest leave this business to us an'—"

But the queer squinted eyes under Torril's hatbrim had been watching her alertly. Now, with neither regard for Flaurity's opinion or for the fact that Flaurity was talking, he put the crux of the matter bluntly:

"That top screw of yours, if you want to know, has got himself another piece o' steak—*see?*"

Flame turned a puzzled look to Flaurity. "Whatever in the world—"

"He means," growled Flaurity harshly, "that yo'r friend has killed another guy."

"My— You mean *Andros?*"

"Yeah. *Andros,*" Torril mocked. "Tonight, just now, he killed Joce Latham."

Plain to see in this moonlight was the startled dismay that paled Flame's cheeks. All caught that sharply indrawn breath —the involuntary gesture that sent one hand to her breast.

Tom Flaurity looked away; but Torril, spurred on by an evident malice, said smugly, "I was there in Latham's place when it happened. I seen it all—an' Bronc did too; he was right there with me. Your range boss was a-shinin' up to Latham's woman an' Latham come in an' caught him. This Andros yanked his gun—Joce didn't have no chance a-tall."

Flame looked at the man with hard, straight eyes. "You're not a clever liar, Bishop. Andros isn't the kind to waste his time on a gambler's woman—"

"I guess," Torril said, scowling away the dark look of his cheeks, "that's what-for he's staying' so long in town, ma'am." He smiled then with a look of amiability. "I expect that's why he's in a back room now with Latham's harlot."

Flame Tarnell's lips came open and she stood that way, eyeing Torril with the hurt bewilderment she might have shown had he slapped her across the mouth. She backed away a stumbling pace, the knuckles of one hand jammed hard against her teeth. With the harsh, crass laugh of Bronc Culebra in her ears, red-cheeked she whirled, making blindly for the house.

8

THE POT CALLS THE KETTLE BLACK

THAT STRANGE peace into which Andros had descended did not, in reality, last longer than a short ten minutes. He regained consciousness in a different room from that in which he'd fallen. There was a strong medicinal smell about him and just over him stood a shirt-sleeved, bearded sawbones. This was 'a room much smaller than the barroom, but that pale-cheeked girl over whom hostilities had started was still close by him. She was tearing some white, flimsy garment into thin strips and watching him with her wide dark eyes across the medico's shoulder.

The doctor straightened with a grunt. "Guess that will— Oh! so you've come out of it, eh? Hurt much? How's your head feel? Kind of light?" He nodded sagely. "You'll get along. You can't kill these damn ranch hands," he told the girl as he pulled the cuffs of his shirt sleeves down. "This boy's got a constitution like an ox."

He looked back at Andros, grinned at him encouragingly. "You'll be all right. Never mind the dizziness—that's a pretty cheap price to pay for the kind of brashness you showed. They tell me you never even ducked. Must think your hide is armor! Stay in bed two weeks and—*What?* You'll do nothing of the sort! You'll stay right where you are, young man, for *at least* two weeks or I'll wash my hands of you. Scowl all you want—I *mean* it!"

Andros got an elbow under him and, despite the doctor's voluble protests, swung to a sitting posture on this couch where he'd been laid. The thing did considerable creaking and he groaned once or twice himself as pain knifed along his ribs again with renewed energy. But he could stand it, he reckoned. He *had to.* There were things that needed doing.

The medico, horrified to see his patient getting up, came rushing over with spluttered wrath, but Andros waved him off.

"No use, Doc," he muttered, fumbling with his shirt buttons. "I know how you feel an' I'm a heap obliged to you. But I've got chores to do an' they ain't waitin' on no blasted two-weeks vacation."

The bandage was a little bulky but he got the shirt buttoned round it. He stood up, reaching a hand to the wall to steady himself. He dug some greenbacks from a pocket and tossed them on the table. "You're fortunate in your patient, Doc. You're goin' to get a lot of advertisin'."

The doctor's stare was incredulous. "Good God, man! You tryin' to underwrite the undertaking business? Do you realize—"

"You bet! That's what I'm gettin' up for."

"You keep flat on your back for the next two weeks or you'll be buried before the first week's over! The human body—"

"Sorry, Doc. The body's mine."

He turned a twisted smile at the girl. "I'm sorry about your trouble—but you saw the play, ma'am. I only did what I had to. You've got your chance now. Go on back East an' leave this country to nuts that are fool enough to like it."

He picked up his cartridge belt and buckled it about him. He took the two big pistols from their sheaths and looked them over critically. He shook their cartridges onto the table and replaced them with fresh ones drawn from his belt.

"You've lost a lot of blood—"

"Sure. Andros returned his guns to leather. He said to the scowling medico: "Nice, meetin' you an' all," and with a ghastly grin shakily started toward the door.

It came open before he got there.

The man behind it was Grave Creek Charlie, boss of the fighting sheepmen. He stopped with his mouth wide open. A glassy look sheared across his stare. And then his eyes bulged frantically.

"Lookin' for somebody?" Andros jeered.

The man seemed frozen in his tracks. Incapable of speech he looked. He shook his head like a pole-axed steer and commenced an impetuous backing.

Andros' cheeks were set and sultry. He dropped his stare to Grave Creek's boots. There was brittle frost in the look he brought up. "Too bad. Your luck's out, sheepman. The bullet ain't been cast that'll send me where you're wishin." Come you're catchin' different notions now's a damn good time to prove it. Turn loose your howl, you sheep dog."

Grave Creek's look was a paralyzed thing. He stood stiff-placed beyond the door; his shadow made a rigid shape across its sunlit sill. There was no motion in him. His eyes clung glassily to Andros' face. He seemed there to read some threat that shook all thought of action out of him. He stood there stunned, gone breathless.

They made a grim, unforgettable picture poised there in this tautened stillness. There was no sound, no movement, in all this plank-walled place.

The tableau was rudely broken.

The swing of slatted doors scratched a harsh sound across the stillness, and a man came in without his hat, one lock of hair between his eyes, his sweating cheeks coarse-streaked with dust. "Rockin' T's callin' a meetin'—"

That many panted words spilled from him before he stopped with jaw loose-hanging, his startled eyes fixed blankly on the smiling cheeks of Andros.

But he was quick. He grasped the play on the instant, and nervously backed three halting steps, his boot-sound like dropped plates in the stealthy quiet. His tongue darted across his dry lips and his desperate glance jumped from Andros' face to Grave Creek's.

"That's quick work," Andros drawled approvingly, and his displayed smile made this newcomer wince and back away another step. "Accurate, too—you're to be commended, Grave Creek, on the speed that keeps you posted."

Then he looked at them derisively. "Make the most of it," he said and wheeled across the room, striding between the rooted sheepmen and crossing the saloon without turning.

He loosed the gelding's reins from the hitchrail and, with the animal in tow, strode down the dusty street with the smashing sun hot upon his back and with shoulders hunched to the pain in him.

He came to the stable and turned in there and dropped his reins to the straw-littered floor. He considered the tall, lean-bodied man who stared at him from the shadows. The man, stepping forward, put his back to a stall post and, from that position, eyed him reticently with his folded arms well away from his belt.

Hay smell and the smell of horses was an acrid thing in this air. It buoyed him. A familiar tang that felt good in his nostrils. He shrugged abruptly. He said to the watching stableman, "This afternoon I had to kill a man. A chore I take no pride in—but a necessary one. You were at Quinn River four years ago. I'm afraid I don't remember you."

The stableman's face showed stolid. "Does it matter?"

"I think it does. It's not often I forget a face." The corners of Andros' mouth grew tight. "Who are you, friend?"

The man's lips showed a thin and reluctant smiling. "They called me Gallup John, them days."

Light broke lines across Andros' cheeks. "The Quinn River marshal!"

The stableman said, "We didn't have very much in common."

"No," Andros said. "I guess we didn't," and felt the stableman's glance trekking after him through the door.

There was something urgent Andros had to do. He felt a need to get in touch with Major Bocart. He had just recalled this gun the Major had given him—this gun rolled snug behind his cantle which had once belonged to Dakota Krell—had belonged, so Bocart had said, to the last man attempting the gun trick which was Bocart's test for applicants.

Andros found it hard to believe Krell could have met his death in two different places, and on two different dates, at that. There was a chance the Major had watched Krell die. If he had not—But, of course, someone other than Krell might have used that gun in the Major's office. Either way, Clem Andros had to know.

From his long knowledge of Krell, and Krell's character, Andros did not think the Major and Dakota Krell had ever met. He was not the kind the Major would hire, with his shifty eyes and cat-thin lips—with his slitted dead-snake stare. It seemed to Andros a deal more likely that some way another man had come into possession of Dakota's pistol, even as Andros himself now had it.

One vague disquiet tightened Andros' cheeks. Despite all evidence to the contrary the man *might* still be alive.

But what Andros wanted badly to know right now was whether or not the man who had brought Krell's pistol into the Major's office with him had been given the same information concerning the Forest movement which Bocard had given him. If he had, it explained a lot of things. The Forest movement's adversaries appeared particularly well informed—which, to Andros' mind, was in no way a healthy condition.

He thought of that dusty hatless man who'd barged into the saloon with the knowledge of Rocking T's called meeting. It had not been later than this very morning that he'd sent the Tarnell punchers out to gather the men for that meeting. If the sheep crowd, knowing when, where and why that meeting was to be called, didn't figure to do something about it, also, there was sure enough something almighty rotten in Denmark!

A new set of plans must be formulated at once. Andros reflected morosely that he was not feeling up to planning much; that nagging pain in his side was engaging too much of his

62

attention. It was sapping his energy, too. It was getting worse again.

His thoughts swung back. It was not like Dakota Krell to go risking his life so foolishly by trying any tricks with a pistol. Even if Krell was alive and mixed up in this infernal sheep-cattle-lumber-railroad-National Forest business, it was not in his character to have done himself what easily he could have hired someone else to do. The man had never been given to the taking of unnecessary risks. He had never been the kind to do *anything* he could get another to do as well.

Dakota Krell had sense.

Andros crossed the windrowed dust of that sun-smoked street and mounted the scarred board porch of Long Rope's lone hotel. Sun-warped, a weatherbitten shack it was, thrown together of native pine whipsawed from the vanished yesterdays. It was garnished with a tall false front intended to convey an impression of three full stories where but one existed in solid fact.

He stepped through the open doorway, getting pen and ink and paper from an observant and reticent proprietor. He went to the table shoved against the farther wall of the small and dusty lobby. The buzz of flies was a steady drone as he eased himself into a stiff-backed chair. He sat awhile there resting, with canted head upon an elbow-propped hand, endeavoring to corral his scattering thoughts.

He roused at last and, staring morosely at the cheap, lined paper, picked up the scratchy pen and began laboriously scrawling hen-tracked words. But the effort of this was tremendous and his thoughts did not come easily. Halfway through he abruptly stopped. The Major would not like this. The last thing Bocart had told him was: "Any jam you get into you can stay in, far as this Service is concerned."

Andros realized then the crazy thing he'd set his hand to. He was not in any jam just yet—but he quickly would be if he tried to post this letter in any town in the Four Peaks country. The new Forest movement's adversaries, Bocart said, had spies all over this country. These men would never permit a stranger's notes. . . .

He tore the letter up and thrust the fragments into a pocket.

The hotel keeper's glance was blandly disinterested when Andros went heavily past him, turning out upon the street.

By his shadow Andros saw the time was hugging five

o'clock. His head felt strangely light again. His skin was clammed with sweat as, feeling the pangs of hunger, he saw a restaurant's sign and willed his rebelling body toward it.

He went in. A long, gaunt place this was, with on one side a clean but fly-harassed counter. The other side was flanked by two long rows of scrubbed-white tables garnished with stiff-backed chairs. There were no customers present when Andros swayed to a stool at the counter.

A man in what once had been a spic-and-span white apron got up off his elbows, laid his cigar on the counter's edge and limped up to get Andros' order.

Andros, when the man had gone, cupped calloused hands to his heated face. There was a faded sign on the wall across from him which said: "Gents learning to spell are politely asked to use last week's paper." He stared at this till the man returned with his supper. Its only merit was heat. Andros ate lethargically and, now that he had got it, without appetite; but he finally cleaned his plate and, leaving the price beside it, got up to go.

He had just climbed off the stool when a shadow fell across the floor and a whiskered old fellow stood peering in. Locating Andros he said: "Miz' Latham wants to see you. She's over at the saloon."

Andros rubbed one hand along the smooth edge of the counter. "Tell Mrs. Latham," he said wearily, "I'll see her next time I come this way." He stood there thoughtful while the old man left, after which he cuffed his hat down over his eyes and tramped out after him. The stabbing pains in his side were worse. He lurched against the restaurant wall and hung there, groggy, till he got his breath. If his enemies had come for him then they could have taken him without resistance. It was all Andros could do to keep himself erect and moving when, finally, he went lurching toward the stable. He staggered like a drunken fiddler, but with jaw grim-set he made it.

The shadows of approaching dusk were thick inside the stable murk. Gallup John came out of the gloom. His glance combed Andros' cheeks intently. He said, "I'll get your bronc. Wait here."

Andros still was waiting when, above the sounds of the stableman's labor, a quick, springy crunch of footsteps wheeled him round to face Grace Latham.

Slanting rain poured earthward from a black and cloud-tossed sky. Through this steady drench of water rode a ponchoed solitary horseman who urged his dark bronc down the last steep pitch of Diamond Mountain and out upon the running flat where huddled the soaked adobes of Half-Circle Arrow's headquarters. It was not two hours since a moon had ridden these heavens; but the roof of the world lay hidden now behind dark layers of curdled cloud, and the stillness of these limitless distances was crammed with the monotone purr of rain, was jarred by the rolling oaths of thunder, was seared and blanched by the threat of lightning's whiplash. The soggy pound of this animal's hoofs was lost in the roaring maelstrom—was found and again torn away by the flapping skirts of a rising gale.

The solitary rider pressed on, unperturbed by rain and wind-lash, indifferent to storm's blustery outbursts, cautious only to catch first sight of other storm-bound travelers.

He swore presently and jerked his horse up sharply, wheeling him into a catclaw thicket and clamping quick hand across the swelling nostrils. For there came other riders, forward-hunched above their saddles, splashing from the yonder lane that led to the outfit's largest building.

When lightning's flare had dimmed away and storm's full darkness had rushed like a wave across the puddled flats, the lone rider turned his mount behind three willow's interlaced branches and there remained until successive flashes proved the flats deserted.

He came then from their cover, a careful man who gave no edge to risk, and swung his own horse into the lane vacated by those other riders. He jogged this trail at a sloshing pace till the heavier blackness of the big house's angles imposed their outlines stark against night's thinner dark.

He pulled to a halt beside the veranda, swung dripping down and dropped his reins. He crossed the porch planks then and sideways passed through a door held open by his own left hand. Barstow, with glance lifted from his cluttered desk, showed a deeper dark in the roan of his cheeks. He came out of his seat with a jarring oath. His bull-throated yell sailed against this man like the flat of an ax. *"Where the hell you think you been?"*

The man's teeth gleamed in a twisted grin while his shoulders made an arcing gesture and his insolent stare quartered Barstow's face with a cold amusement. It was the only answer Barstow got.

"I told you to get here *yesterday! Didn't I?*"

Barstow took two forward steps. His fists were clenched and his lamp-thrown shadow was a monstrous blotch against the wall. A huge and lumbering beast he looked as he crouched there with his face contorted and tried to make the other quail. "You cocky bastard!" The hurled-out words were ugly, gritted. "I ought to smash that goddam grin down your throat!"

With lips still curved the man, without fear, drew the makings out of a dry vest pocket. When the smoke was rolled his glance came up. He leered at the Half-Circle Arrow boss knowingly.

"Y'u got fists," he drawled, "could hammer a man 'most near to death, I reckon—if y'u c'ld ever git 'em on 'im. But don't put on no dawg with me. Y'u couldn't cut it, Barstow."

Breath rushed shrilly through Barstow's teeth. His livid cheeks were mottled, bloated. He showed the desire so rampant in him, the hot wild lust to maim and batter. But he checked his impulse, held his place; rooted there by the man's indifference.

The newcomer chuckled. He kicked the door shut, put his back against it while rain from his poncho pooled the floor about his muddy boots.

He was tall—very near as tall as Barstow, but without the rancher's brawny bigness. Rather, he was lithe, slim waisted, quick and sure in all his movements. Brash were the eyes beneath his hatbrim, hard was the mouth above his rakish jaw.

He crossed the room toward Barstow coolly, helped himself to a cigar from Barstow's pocket, snapping his own smoke into a corner. Glaring, Barstow strode quick after it, stamping it out with visible venom. The other man's eyes looked after him, mocking.

He bit the end from his purloined smoke and snapped a match alight on his thumbnail. "Y'u wanted me here for somethin' besides glarin'. S'pose y'u spill it."

Barstow's temper had cramped his style. It had thinned his broad features and squeezed the stare of his amber eyes to pale and wicked-glinting slits. But he could not cringe this man with anger; he had tried before and been derisively

66

laughed at. This dripping man enjoyed his rages. "One day you'll go too far!" he snarled.

"But not today," the fellow chuckled.

With tremendous effort Barstow smoothed his cheeks into some semblance of the other's grin. "I guess we understand each other—"

"C'mon—get at it."

Barstow's scowl was black. "I had a meeting here tonight. If you had—"

"Meetin's bore me," the other man said. "Long's yore backers pay off, I'm for y'u. When they don't I'll find somethin' else. I ain't much worried. Y'u'll see they pay me if y'u value yore health." His smile was malignant. "We savvy each other all right."

But Barstow was not to be tripped again. He kept the hatred off his cheeks and put his mind to his need of this man. The storm had quit, gone rampaging elsewhere, but wind still plucked its cold shrill whine from the swaying trees.

While Barstow shaped his thoughts the dripping rider whistled the dust from a nearby chair and eased his lean wet form down into it. Muddied water marked his trail from the door. Barstow's glance morosely eyed it.

He said gruffly, "The sheep'll be back here in three-four weeks. Was kind of scared till we got this rain; but they'll come now. Soon's the grass gets up—what they've left, I mean. Talmage allows they'll be crossin' over ninety-five thousan' head through the Four Peaks country. Says it looks like Roosevelt'll lick us on this Forest business; it's in Talmage's mind to clean these two-bit brush-poppers out before the bill goes through."

"I coulda guessed that much without comin' down here," drawled the visitor fleeringly, and pulled back his poncho to puff on a star that was pinned to his vest. He polished the metal with the tail of a curtain. "Some of your brush-poppers is goin' to fight—I s'pose y'u know that? Y'u an' Talmage an' some of them others has whittled this country down to where it ain't got much left to lose. They'll git their backs up this time."

"They've got their backs up now," Barstow said. "I got the word not half an hour back. Rockin' T's called a meetin' at the Flowerpot for tomorrow night. They've sent invites to Boxed Q, Tadpole, Spur an' Lazy J."

The man in the chair merely shrugged indifferently.

Scowling, Barstow said, "Which'll be when we smash 'em." He purred with satisfaction: "We'll hit that meetin' like a load of logs! Grave Creek's camped with twenty men just north of town; with them an' my fourteen we'll give hell some helpers. I want you to stay in town where—"

" 'D y'u get me out here to tell me that?"

"I got you out here to show you how to run your job."

The lean star-packer sneered. "When I take lessons off'n y'u—"

Barstow snarled, "The way you gallivant about this country it's a whoppin' wonder you ever *do* know what's goin' on! For a marshal you sure don't grow no moss around Long Rope! The Rockin' T's got a new range boss—"

"That ain't news; it always gettin' one. Reg'lar as clockwork, every month."

"The one it's got now is news," snapped Barstow, "an' don't you doubt it! This guy blew Cranston's light with just one puff. This noon he killed Joce Latham in his own saloon. God only knows what he's doin' now!"

But Long Rope's marshal was no longer listening. Straightened in his chair his look was suddenly intent—pleased and thoughtful and wholly busied with something in mind. His eyes showed a lewd and febrile gleaming. He ran a moist tongue across his lips and, getting up, cuffed his wet hat to a rakish angle.

He grinned. "I guess that leaves Joce's woman—"

"You eave that damn slut out of this! You listen to what I'm tellin' you!" Barstow swung the words at the man like cudgels. "You'll get hamstrung by a dame yet, dam you! But you'll do it on your own time—*get me?* You lose us this game—"

"Ahr! Get on with it," Long Rope's marshal told him. "Jest strip it down an' never mind preachin'. What about the Rockin' T squirt?"

"I kinda thought you might mebbe know him. His name," Barstow said, "is Black Clem Andros."

The marshal went dead still in his tracks. His face went pale as wood ash and he looked at Barstow and never saw him. All the cocky confidence was gone clean out of him. He seemed to age ten years in that moment.

He spoke no word; and Barstow said: "I see you do!"

The marshal jerked and his eyes were frantic. Hoarse, blasphemous oaths came tumbling out of him and he paced the room like a captured tiger. He was cursing still when the door shoved open and Bishop Torril came sloshing in with Bronc Culebra.

A watchful glint colored Torril's stare. "How are you, Krell? Long time no see. How's the star-packin' business comin' these days?"

Culebra sneered. "By the look of his pan someone's swiped his star—or mebbe his woman! That *would* be good! The biter bit!" He laughed uproariously and all by himself. The sound quit suddenly as Krell's tall shape went into a crouch.

Culebra cried hastily: "Wait, Krell—wait I meant no off—"

"One mo' crack outa y'u an' I'll put y'u in a coffin!" Like the glint of his teeth, Krell's voice was wicked. "Y'u two bums come in here fo' somethin'—spill it an' git!"

Smoothly Bishop Torril said, "Andros got nicked in that shoot-out with Latham." He directed the words at Barstow, adding: "Thought mebbe you might want to know that."

Barstow nodded. His mind was still on Krell's strange conduct. It was the first time he'd ever seen Dakota Krell scared.

"Well," Torril said, "we figured they'd be plantin' him, come mornin'. Grave Creek rode up an' when he heard about it he allowed he aimed to go in an' spit in the face of corpse number two—meanin' Andros. He grabbed open the door an' liked to die of shock. Me, too! There was this Andros up on his hoofs an' comin' towards us like the wrath of Gawd! Right then, Bill Lovin' come bustin' in all lathered up an' spoutin' about that meetin' Rockin' T's called at the Flowerpot. He stopped, quick's he seen Andros standin' there. Andros says: 'Make the most of it!'—"

"All right," snarled Krell. "Y'u've spilled yo' guts. Now dust."

Torril, in the quiet that crept about them, pulled himself two inches straighter. His turning gaze was soft, misleading. But that brown and drooping mustache neither concealed nor in any way glossed over the long and tight compression of his mouth.

"Playin' this game," he drawled, "is bound to brush a man's elbows again' a pretty broad stripe of skunk—but he ain't obliged to take lip off'n 'em."

It was Dakota Krell's glance that slid away.
"Git out! Git out " he gritted.

9

COMPLICATIONS

IN THE stable gloom Andros faced the girl.

He could see the surge of her breasts against the fabric of her tinseled bodice and in the hush her breathing made a hurried, husky whisper. He could glimpse the drawn expression of her cheeks, and their high pallor. Then she was close against him, one hand tightly gripping his arm.

"Andros!" she breathed softly. "Andros—don't leave this town tonight. Don't go!"

"They're expectin' me at the Rockin' T, ma'am—"

"Of course. I know. Of course they'll be expecting you. But don't you *see?* Those men that were in the saloon—they'll lay for you on the trail. They were Latham's friends. They—they'll kill you!"

"I reckon not."

"But they will! I saw it in their eyes!" she wailed. "You're sick—you're hurt—you wouldn't stand a chance! *Please!* For my sake, Andros— *Andros!* My God, boy, don't . . ."

Even through this gloom Andros could see the redness of her lips, the starry, widesprung darkness of her eyes. A mighty handsome girl she was, intelligent and sensitive. Andros could not blame Latham for his jealousy.

But he shook his head. "I'm sorry, ma'am—sorry for everything. But I've got to go—"

"No! *No!*" she cried, and her glance was frantic. "You'll be—"

"I'll have to chance that, ma'am."

Her hand fell from his arm. A great weariness bowed her pale bare shoulders; he could feel the courage drain out of her. She stood silent, with all her muscles slack and with her stare gone helplessly through the open window into night's collecting shadows. It was as though unavailingly she had tried to grasp and hold some thing she knew she could never capture. Her breasts were stilled. She was beside him,

70

scarcely breathing, and Andros saw with a sudden clarity the bitter nature of her aloneness.

They stood a bare three feet apart. The girl had pluck; it was a remembered quality he recalled discerning at San Carlos the night he'd knocked Latham down in the restaurant. She had pluck; but it was now a conviction of her helplessness that stirred him strongest. He wanted to comfort her, to reassure her, but stood silent, abashed by the knowledge that a single word from him would do it—a word he could never give.

Her voice reached out to him softly. "Isn't there anything—?"

He shook his head. "I couldn't do it, ma'am; it wouldn't mean anything—you wouldn't want it that way. You'd hate me an' I'd hate myself. A man's got to live according to his lights."

She stood there, still as death, looking outward into the thickening gloom. She appeared to be pondering his words. And then she whipped around; stood facing him. In her lifted eyes was a strange intentness. It might have been the reflection of some hard and reached decision. Abruptly, inexplicably, looking up at him that way she smiled. "People *are* queer, aren't they? Shall I tell you something? That first night —that night I saw you in San Carlos; remember?—I said, 'Here comes the man I've always dreamed of. . . .' Odd, isn't it? When I was a little girl I lived on a farm in the Missouri bottoms. I used to climb an old tree there and sit and think for hours. What air castles I used to build! I had grand notions; I was going to be a circus queen!"

She laughed a little, wistfully; and Andros smiled.

"I used to dream that some day I would meet the finest man— a tall man, lean and handsome, who would come and woo me like some knight of old and carry me off on his big roan gelding. And, finally, I met a man. Tall, and in his way quite handsome . . . and very artful. And he *did* carry me off. I ran away with him and married him and . . . when I woke up I *hated* him. He made my life a hell for months. Until you came, and killed him, and I realized, too late, it was you that I had dreamed of."

Wistfulness, a forlorn mad passion, lay dangerously near the surface of those final soft-breathed words. Andros could feel the tug and vibrance of her. It was on his lips to say

71

something about Joce Latham when he saw the turn of her shoulders loosen, saw her shrug as Joce himself might have done; a gambler's shrug, concealing much or little.

No words would come to Andros' call when he saw her rueful smiling.

Perhaps she expected none. "Well, thanks for listening," she said abruptly, and took a long, deep breath, as though putting that part behind her. "I thought I'd got all over day-dreaming."

She moved closer, near enough for him to have put quick arms about her. The firm, warm pulsing of her breasts was against him briefly. She said: "Andros—do you really care so much for her?"

"Mebbe you better ride that trail again, ma'am."

"Flame Tarnell, I mean. You're working for her—they say you're Rocking T's new range boss." Her glance was grave, and melancholy was a shading in her voice that touched him with a deep despair. "You were a fool to cross Grave Creek Charlie. Tell me true; do you find her so attractive, Andros?"

Andros' cheeks felt hot and flushed. "Why, ma'am," his tone held protest, "you're sure imaginin' things—"

She shook her head. "I'm afraid not. Did I imagine I heard you telling those men no more sheep would cross this Four Peaks country? You were crazy to have told them that. That you should have wanted them stopped I can understand; but to *warn* them that way of your intentions— Red Hat will never rest till he has driven you out or killed you. I know him, Andros. Is Flame Tarnell *worth* such terrible risk?"

Andros had no answer to that and his glance strayed uncomfortably toward the thickened gloom of the stable's rear. It was high time Gallup John was getting done with that saddling. He felt a mighty wish the man would hurry. This girl kept talk beyond his depth. It embarrassed him that she could be so personal. Frankness ceased to be a virtue when shoved that way at a man.

Nor was she done. Her voice came softly, pleading; her hand pulled him round to face her. "Andros!" It was a wail almost, the way she said it. "What has Flame Tarnell to offer that I can't give you better? What—"

He said in desperation. "You're talkin' wild-like, ma'am. You've got this whole play figured wrong. Flame Tarnell owns the ranch I'm roddin'—there's nothin' between us personal!

72

How *could* there be? I'm nothin' but a crazy, driftin' gun-packer—a Salt River ranny with no past a man could talk about an' a mighty sight less in the way of prospects. I'd have no business travelin' double harness even if I was the marryin' kind—which I ain't. Get that foolishness out of your head. This is just a chore—"

"Do you always put such energy into your chores?" she cut dryly. "Is it your habit to let men shoot you and then, when you'd ought to be flat on your back with fever, to go hunting up more enemies so as to give them on a platter the chance . . ." Her voice trailed off with bitter hoplessness. Abruptly, soft and completely pleading, she said: "Oh Andros—"

"Ma'am," he blurted, "you oughtn't talk like that!"

Change ran its darkness through her eyes. She swayed as though whatever cane she'd used to bolster courage now had snapped. Haggard lines of weariness marked her cheeks. The dull indifference of her listless voice depressed him immeasurably. "Why don't you say it?" she asked drearily. "Why don't you tell me I'm a no good slut?"

To hear such talk from this young girl's lips, to see them twisting so bitterly, was more than he could stand. Her words had bitten deep into him and, hardly himself knowing what he meant to do, he was starting toward her when she whirled and, with a queer, choked sob, plunged blindly into the night.

With glance unutterably miserable, with the planes of his high cheeks gone dark and taciturn, Black Clem Andros let her go. There was vast pity in him and a wealth of sympathy, for he understood what was in her mind. But such things could not be, with him. There was nothing he could do for her. Too well he knew that, bitterly.

Gallup John strode from the blackness with no expression on his face and handed him the reins of his saddled horse. He thrust them, unspeaking, into Andros' hands and wheeled away immediately.

Andros stared uncomprehendingly after him, feeling dissatisfied with himself and little knowing what to do about it, and at last got into his saddle.

In the living-room of Barstow's ranch headquarters, these four men for some while stood absolutely still. Krell's dark face was demoniac. He raised his shaking fists. "Get out! God damn you—*git!*"

One longer moment Torril eyed him, then turned upon his heel contemptuously and started, with Bronc Culebra following, toward the door.

Krell's hand was one streaked blur of light. Down and up it leaped, and flame jumped from the gleaming tube that showed beyond his knuckled grip. The shot's report rose huge and thunderous.

Torril's spinning body jerked. The hinges of his knees collapsed and dropped him in a crumpled heap.

A hot breath hissed through Culebra's teeth. His slitted eyes were glittering cracks of hate and wild, hot anger. With ash-gray cheeks his body crouched with clawed hands spread above gun butts.

But the feline sneer on Krell's thin lips was mad and wicked as the glow of his eyes. He had one hand still whitely wrapped about the stock of his leveled gun; its gaping muzzle was fixed point-blank on Culebra's chest.

"Are you wantin' some?" he jeered.

* * *

Andros' eyes came painfully open on a room he had never seen before; a room entirely unfamiliar. A single window, dead before him, poured in a flood of warm and lazy light that dappled the sparse and roundabout furnishings with spots of gold that, by their placement, proved the time to be late afternoon.

He was not out of his head, though he had for a moment thought so. His faculties were sufficiently clear to tell him he was in a pine-slat bunk, and its position against one rough log wall was proof he was in a cabin. Some line rider's shack, was his natural thought.

He heard no sound of movement and guessed that he was alone in the place. He lay there quiet for many minutes, absorbing such details as came to view; striving to piece together the forgotten acts that had brought him to this situation.

The dusty floor showed scuffed boot tracks where the litter of broken and discarded gear left any place for foot room. A warped table in the corner held a miscellany of things, the sort of stuff rannies cram in their warsacks; wrinkled underwear tangled with a washed and unwashed smear of socks, a shaving outfit in a leather case, a latigo strap draped over a pair of go-to-hell shirts, a dog-eared tally book, a spool of

74

thread and a packet of rusty needles. An old hat drooped from a peg on the wall.

There was a door at the room's far end and, like the window before him, it stood open. The view disclosed was of shadowed pines with, beyond, the sharp pitch of a timbered slope.

But this told him little, for there was plenty of that kind of country roundabout, he guessed. He saw nothing from which he could compute a notion of his whereabouts.

His faculties were closely taken up with this, for he keenly felt the need of knowledge; but there was a portion of his mind rather irritably striving to connect his being here with what had gone before.

He remembered leaving town. It had been dark at the time. It was almost dark again; therefore it must have been yesterday that he left the ranch to ride into that gun-smoke trouble with Latham. But he had left town; he could plainly recall riding out of it after that embarrassing talk with Grace Latham. He remembered that, and the shot that had whistled past within feel of his ear just after he'd put Long Rope behind. He had ridden and ridden for what seemed hours; but he must have dozed or have been but partly conscious, for this recollection was a hazy thing—disjointed. There was much that had happened after for which he could not account. He had seemed to have been burning up; his veins had writhed with some strange malignant heat, and his limbs had got unwieldy. He remembered how the moon had fled. He recalled the steady roar of the rain, the grateful feel of it soaking him and its impotence to quench the conflagration in his veins. He had a dim thought he must have fallen from his horse.

And that was all.

What events had shaped after that he did not know, nor how he had come here, nor where this was.

He pondered it for quite a while with the buzz of circling flies for accompaniment and the tang of the pines smelling good in his nostrils. Then he saw his clothes on the floor by the table and realized he must be undressed. He hoisted the blanket and peered beneath it to find that another bandage had been added to the one the Doc had bound on him. There was an unpleasant smell to the blanket. Some odor he knew but

75

could not place. He judged this might be a nester's shack and, conjecturing, he dozed.

When he woke again his head was clear. His mind was sharper and a deal of the pain had gone from his side. He felt hungry now and thought considerably about getting up and pawing round to find what sort of food was here. But he slumped down off his elbow quickly. The sweat of that exertion took a long time drying.

He was not as tough as he had figured. And this was odd. He'd been shot plenty times before and never felt so kitten weak.

But he was definitely awake now and his mind got busy. Sunlight, smashing through that window with a renewed brilliance, proved this morning. Another night had gone down the back trail.

He had not been alone all the time he slept, for the yonder door was closed now and there was a spoon and a greasy dish upon the floor nearby. Evidently someone had fed him some kind of broth. Broth! They must believe he was pretty sick. His roving glance observed a bright and cared-for rifle, a .30.30, now standing against the table.

These things he noted subconsciously. His mind was busy with other matters. Such as how he'd better be sending someone to warn the Flowerpot; and how Flame Tarnell would sure be wondering where he'd gone to.

And, thinking of Flame, he thought of other things concerning her! the lithe and supple shadow that she made against the sun, the sound of her voice through changing moods, the courageous spirit and that rugged honesty that shone so patent from all her features. He loved the play of the light in her hair, its midnight blackness and sleek blue luster. It was in his mind some man would win a precious thing in her.

He mused awhile, thus dreaming.

Somehow then his shifting thoughts wheeled his mind to the girl, Grace Latham. A gambler's woman. Grace Latham . . . She had pluck, and something finer he would not let her waste on him. He regretted that it was not in him to be of any use to her, that his capacities did not include the chance of his ever loving her; for he had sensed in her a fullness and strong possibilities for betterment if the right man mated up with her—but he was not that man. They traveled different

76

trails, she and him. A matter of mental viewpoint, perhaps. Each sought a goal beyond attainment; this was what they had in common—the only thing. It was not enough. He saw with clarity the forlornness of her hopes and his, the crass futility of their strivings. Man was born to a course laid out before he was conceived. That which was to be would be; what was not written, no man's efforts could persuade. This was the truth Black Andros had learned from twenty-three years of living.

He sighed, knowing the attraction he possessed for Grace; and sighed the harder for knowing where his own wish lay— for knowing, too, how little could ever come of it. Better far that he and Flame should never meet again.

He had set his hand to violence and could not cut loose of it now. A king of hammer-bangers whom a lesser breed took joy in hunting, when it dared. That members of that glory-loving tribe seldom found that much pure courage, was beside the point; he was a pistol-grabber who was almost legend, and was so marked. He could take no woman into that kind of life. Yet he could not swerve his thoughts from realization that Flame Tarnell would one day be the end of some man's trail.

She'd be the end of his, he knew well enough, if he didn't get her out of mind. You could not mix day-dreams and gunplay.

His thoughts were abruptly terminated by the sound of a crunching boot. It came from beyond the door and, looking that way, Andros saw it open, letting in a gush of sunlight swiftly blocked by the man's black shape. The man stepped in and lounged there eying him. A man in boots and chaps that showed hard usage. There was a scraggle of beard on his hard, burnt face. He wore a low-crowned, broad-rimmed hat and packed a sixshooter in tied-down holster.

He had the look, but he was not a cowman.

Andros knew in that short moment what this smell was on his blanket.

THE MESSAGE

FLAME TARNELL, despite herself, thought much of Andros in the days that followed his departure and Bishop Torril's harsh indictment. Again and again Flame told herself Clem Andros was not the kind of man who had been painted by Barstow's foreman. One fact, though, could not be gotten round. If Andros had found no attraction in the Latham woman's charms why hadn't he returned? He might at least have sent some message. Even a lame excuse, she told herself, was better than none at all.

Day followed dragging day and no word came from him, nor of him. She was too proud to seek out word of him in town; her own men might have given some explanation of his absence had she not been too self-conscious of the feelings he had roused in her to ask. Time crawled and the work got done, but Rocking T was not the place it had been. The glow was gone clean out of it.

Two days ago, determined that Andros had indeed forsaken the job that he had asked for, she had made Tom Flaurity range boss. Tom had joined the outfit just before her father's death. A top hand in every sense, his extreme taciturnity had not made him over-popular and he had got the name of living beneath his hat. There was this, and there were other things that made her doubtful of the wisdom of promoting him. The odd way he sometimes regarded her when he figured she was not looking. There was the toughness of his way with the other cowboys . . . the way he handled horses. Yet, in him, there were attributes of leadership; and so, while not completely trusting him, she had—lacking stauncher stuff—named him boss in the departed Andros' stead.

But all Flame's thoughts were of the absent man. She could not help, looking round her, comparing the place to the way it had been during Andros' so-brief tenure. Andros' presence had brought a new and siren song to her; had colored all her actions and thrust a strange exhilaration upon her that was like some heady wine; it had brought her out of herself and into a vivid, exciting world she had not known existed. Somehow, it seemed, he had shown her how to live, had given her an awakening glimpse of the joy that from true living might be gotten. About the man was an atmosphere, intangible yet intriguing; lusty—a veritable tonic that toned up sluggish blood and filled one with a keen pulsating eagerness, endowing the most forlorn of hopes with the gay regalia of certainty.

He was like some great retaining wall that, soaring into the heavens, kept out the clouds and was impregnable as the secrets God had stored in Davy Jones' locker. In Andros she had sensed that tremendous, unassuming confidence that complements completest knowledge of the frailties of humankind and of oneself, the kind of wisdom locked within an old man's heart.

She had read into some of his actions the taints of callousness, of cynicism and contempt; yet deep within the man himself she had sensed better things convincing her at soul he was a vital force for good—or could be, if he had someone to point the way. She was convinced of the sterling qualities he had screened behind that shell of cynical toughness he presented to the world. That calm tranquility he so usually showed, the very bitterness that seemed so strong a part of him—these combined to reveal him in her mind an extraordinarily colorful, dynamic figure.

The low and muted thud of hoofs from some place yonder presently pulled her from her thoughts. Glancing up, looking out across the wind-ruffled surface of the tank, looking past its farthest edge of cracked and hooftracked gumbo to where the range stretched seared and yellow, she saw the rider. A faint frown put pinched lines between her brows as she watched his leisurely progress. He was riding slow, being careful of his horse in the furnace heat of this midday sun. She was certain she did not know the man. He did not look like a grubline rider. He came with a purpose she was sure, and unaccountably, as she watched him ride in past the tank, there crept over her a premonition of disaster.

She glanced worriedly toward the bunkhouse. None of the crew was in sight, but Tom Flaurity's big bay stood saddled before the foreman's shanty and Flame breathed easier for knowing she was not alone.

Beside the porch the rider stopped. He did not trouble to remove his hat but sat there looking down at her with the thoughts behind his sloe-black eyes inscrutable. He was a little man whose swarthy face was adorned with lean, pinched features.

She left her chair and crossed to the porch-edge, facing him. She looked to read the brand on his horse and saw the man's tight lips quirk faintly. His pony bore no brand; there was dried sweat upon its flanks beneath the crusted dust.

Flame studied the man's face thoughtfully.

He said, "I guess y'u are Miz' Tarnell?"

She nodded.

"I got a note fer y'u," he grunted, fumbling in a pocket. The hand came presently to sight again, and he held out to her a soiled scrap of blue-lined paper obviously torn from someone's tally book.

She took it nervously and read it. With throat gone dry she read again:

Am bad hurt and holed up some place south of Boulder Mountain. Send some food if you can by man who brings this message. Don't come out yourself.

There was neither heading nor signature, but sick at heart Flame knew at once whose hand had scrawled the message. Her cheeks were hot, her veins like ice. She put a hand out weakly to support herself against a post lest this sharp-eyed rider see the shaking of her knees.

"Who gave you this?" she asked when she could trust her voice. "Describe him."

"Well—" the fellow hesitated, rasped a hand across his stubbled jaw. "The gent wasn't givin' out his handle an' he wasn't the kind y'u'd ask such things of. He was sort of tall, a long-geared ranny, kinda wide across the wind. High, flat mug about the color of my saddle. Smoky eyes an' tough as they come—y'u might think a little tougher." He rubbed his jaw and said: "Flagged me over an' said I was to give this note to y'u. Personal. Don't y'u know who sent it?"

His eyes were on her slyly; and she turned her flushed face thankfully when Flaurity came up. The strange rider could not see him, but he said swift and soft, admonishingly: "Leave that fella out of this. I'll wait y'u on the Edwards Park trail

80

where it dips towards Boulder Creek. Don't forget the grub
. . ." His voice trailed off as Flaurity stopped beside the porch.

Flaurity's voice was unfavorable as his look. "What's this
hombre wantin', ma'am?"

The man turned in his saddle then and said with a cool
contempt: "What'd y'u think I'm after, eh? Her money or
'er life?"

"I ain't thinkin'. Spill it quick an' hit the trail."

"I'm in no hurry. I want a job——"

"You'll get no job around here. Pull out."

The rider's lip curled fleeringly. His mean little eyes peered
at the girl. "What's this stinkin' scissors-bill——"

"Mosey!" Flaurity said real soft.

The swarthy rider turned his mount. He said across his
shoulder: "I wouldn't shame my hawse by bein' found on this
spread."

Flaurity stood, a wiry, angular, menacing shape against
the sun's bright slanting. He watched that way with stiff-set
cheeks till the stranger dropped down into a wash. To Flame
he said then, "This country's needin' a clean-up bad; all sorts
of riff-raff runnin' loose——"

He stopped, amazedly finding himself alone when he looked
round for her. Scowling he eyed the half-closed door leading
into the house. His cheeks showed sultry color. Then he
shrugged and spat and headed, growling beneath his breath,
for the harness shed.

Flame, from back of a window, watched till he went inside.
She emerged then, softly, swiftly crossing the porch and, skirting the tank's near side, hurriedly made her way to the mess
shack. From the stealth with which she entered it one would
never have guessed she owned this ranch and everything upon
it. Very softly, with an immense and foreign care, she closed
its door. She meant to follow the rider's orders to the letter.
Flaurity, the man had said, must not be brought into this.

She left the mess shack ten minutes later with a bundle
under her arm. She went to the stable and got her horse.
The saddling gave her difficulty; she seemed all thumbs and
everything appeared to be conspiring to delay her. She undid
her bundle, disclosing neat-wrapped packets that were hurriedly thrust in her saddlebags. She was leading her pony
toward the door when sound of voices pulled her up.

81

Leaving the horse on grounded reins she crept to the door, paused there tensely while she listened with hammering pulses.

Flaurity's voice said suspiciously: "What you wantin' her for?"

Someone laughed. A man's hard tones said roughly: "Get her out here an' quit arguin' with the law!"

The law! Flame felt faintness stealing over her. She fought it back with all her will—with every resource of her strong young body. They must be after Andros; he had killed a man in town—a gambler, Bishop Torril had said. If, somehow, they had discovered that Andros, hurt and somewhere hiding, had sent that stranger to ask her aid, she would need all her wits about her. She must be careful; a single false move might cost Andros his life. They must not guess the tumult their presence here had roused in her. She must rid the place of them swiftly so she could get this food to where the man— Lord God! if she shou'd miss him . . .

She stifled a shudder—dared not think of that.

She stepped out into the sun's hot smash, striving to appear indifferent to the three men sitting saddles yonder insolently eying Flaurity.

From a corner of her eye she caught the sudden turning of their heads.

Flaurity called: "There's some rannies here to see you, ma'am. They allow their business is a heap important. Mebbe you better talk to them—but don't if you don't want to."

She turned then, fully, looking quietly toward them as though constrained by nothing stronger than an idle curiosity. She hoped the three men thought it that, and fought to still her nerves and oust the fluttering that was in her, to ca'm her agitation lest they see and guess her secret. She tried to face them as Clem Andros would, at ease and coolly tranquil.

Seeing she meant to come no nearer they swung their horses toward her with gaunt Flaurity at their stirrups, belligerence disturbing the set of his freckled features.

They stopped ten paces from her, holding their horses with commands from their knees. From this closer vantage she could see the grip of an excited admiration suddenly coloring and focusing the brash gaze of their leader.

She felt new warmth steal across her cheeks and the leader

grinned. He muttered something about being 'born to blush unseen' and his two companions sniggered.

Flaurity snarled: "That's packin' it far enough, Krell. You've had yore fun. Get down to business or get yore plug-uglies outa here." And he set one hand upon his belt where its fingers brushed his holster.

Krell, a tall lean man with a star, ignored him. His look, and the sleek, quick grace of his movements were remindful of a mountain cat's. His mouth was hard above a rakish jaw and his chin-strapped hat was cuffed at a swaggerish slant across one saturnine eyebrow.

He caught her glance amusedly and doffed the hat with an impudent flourish, bowing low above his saddle. "I'm Sheriff Krell," he said with broad smile, "an' y'u, of course, are Flame Tarnell. I blush to think we've not been acquainted sooner. But a sheriff's duties—" and here he sighed— "sure keep a fella humpin'."

"Of course," she said; and wondered at the evenness of her voice. "Won't you come in and rest awhile? I'm sure the cook—"

"Why, ma'am, that's downright handsome of y'u," Krell said smoothly. "Happens, though, I'm here on business and ain't got a heap of time. We'll leave that pleasure for another day—y'u bet I won't forget it." Still smiling he swung down from the saddle, left his horse on trailing reins.

He looked taller now—tall, almost, as Clem Andros. Thinking of Andros that way helped to calm her trepidation, but she kept her glance upon him, daring not to look away lest he should sense the fright and dismay she was trying so hard to hide from him. "Business . . .?" she said it doubtfully as though she'd no idea what business he could have with her. "I'm afraid we haven't any cattle for sale—"

"It's not that kind of business that's brought me out here, ma'am—an' no one could regret it more than I do. But I've got my duty an' I sure hev got to do it. A complaint has reached me, ma'am, that y'u folks here been stirrin' up trouble, been figurin' to keep the sheep from crossin' back this summer. I been told y'u been connivin' with Spur an' Tadpole, with Lazy J an' some other spreads to organize a vigilance committee."

The glance he put on his deputies brought each man's head around to nod in solemn agreement.

83

"Things like that cause trouble, ma'am. Y'u ain't cravin' to see blood flow, are you? 'Course y'u ain't—no more than me. I can savvy how y'u been feelin' about these sheep. Blasted nuisance. Ruinashun of the range, they are; I feel the same myself about 'em. But law is law, an' right is on their side jest now. Ain't nothin' we can do about it—y'u nor me nor nobody else. Them sheep got as much right to the grass—"

"As a sheepherder's got in heaven," Flaurity said with comprehension.

A lazy grace marked Krell's slow turning, "*Yo'* chance of heaven is sure goin' to be mighty certain if y'u don't shut that mouth."

He swung back, smiling easily, the rolling of his shoulders ·eflecting his low opinion of the Rocking T range boss. He continued smoothly, "Like I was saying, ma'am, we can't hev y'u folks stirrin' up no trouble. Election's comin' on, y'u know, an' honest folks is goin' to be needin' all the votes we can get 'em. Range wars is dam bad medicine—ruin business, knocks politics to hell, an' gets wound up with a lot of faces missin'. Y'u know what come of tryin' to buck sheep last year. We don't want no more of that.

"Now I been told yo' foreman has been shootin' off his jaw in town. Said the Rockin' T was takin' measures t' see that no more sheep crossed through here. That talk's plumb crazy! Y'u couldn't no more stop 'em than the devil could make a snowball. Likewise, it's been pointed out to me that y'u hev called a meetin' at Flowerpot."

Krell's cheeks showed bland and smooth as silk. "I'm warnin' y'u to call that meetin' off right now."

Flame eyed him hotly, all her fears forgotten in her sudden indignation. "You know very well there'll be no meeting called at Flowerpot!" she charged bitterly. "You know that ranch was raided and burnt four nights ago—the night that meeting was supposed to have been held. Only Andros' disappearance kept those plans from going through; if that meeting had been held there'd be a different story going the rounds about that raid! Teal's two hands would be alive tonight and Teal would still be round here instead of run off into the brush!"

"Shucks," smiled Krell, "y'u are gettin' all het up, ma'am." He eyed her with a gleaming mockery. "I ain't surprised yo' foreman pulled his pin fo' other parts. I been huntin' that ranny a right long spell an' over consid'rable country. 'F he sets any value on his hide y'u shore hev seen the last of him."

Flame drew herself up stiffly. "Clem Andros is no outlaw. If he were here you'd not dare call him one!"

Krell laughed. "I won't be callin' no lady a liar, ma'am—special one as pretty as y'u are. Shucks! Long as he keeps away from here y'u'll hev no quarrel with me."

He sobered then. His glance rested on her searchingly. "That Flowerpot raid is sure news to me. Seems like folks hereabouts does all their behavin' when I'm round, an' quick's I ain't makes ready to lift hell plumb off its hinges. I been away the las' two weeks on business; been up Ashdale way to see a couple fellas—"

"About a horse, I guess!"

Her scornful tone appeared to bother Krell not at all. He grinned broadly, showing his teeth. "Well, yes, it was. A sorrel horse," he added and the two men with him guffawed.

"If you'd been here tending to your duty—"

"Y'u are dead right, ma'am. I aim to be, from here on out. I sure feel some constrained about that Flowerpot business. I'll be lookin' into it, y'u bet, though I don't guess I can do much now."

"As if you ever *would* do anything to help an honest rancher!" Flame saw the change film across his glance and would have shut her lips on further talk but for the hot resentment pushing her. "That star you pack does not deceive the honest people round here; we know you for the railroad's spy! A man don't have to run with sheep and cattle kings to show which side of his bread is butttred. Not since you've been in office have you once lifted hand to favor a small independent! Everything you've ever done has been an abomination!"

Rash words were those and fully meant. Flame's eyes blazed her scorn of him. Krell's look was coldly saturnine, bright with malicious humor.

It infuriated Flame beyond discretion. "If you weren't backed by the Pool," she accused, "how could you be holding down two star-packing jobs at once? How could you be Long Rope's marshal and Gila County's sheriff?" She took a long, deep breath and said: "I think I'll ask Reb Barstow what he thinks about your politics!"

"That's a right smart notion, ma'am," Krell drawled. "Yes,

sir," he said, swinging up into his saddle with a feline grin,
' Y'u do jest that, ma'am, will y'u? Meantime I'll be leavin'
these two deputies on yo' place to see y'u don't go to startin'
somethin' that might jest mebbe someway embarrass Reb—
or get yo'self in trouble."

11

RED HAT

FLAME bit her lip as she stood there staring after him. She
was a fool to let her temper drive her into hurling such rash
words at him. She had put the man on guard. She had made
an enemy of the man who represented all the law there was
in this country. A man who would not forget—the timbre of
that laugh proclaimed it.

She put a hand to her forehead wearily; it was a worried
gesture that pushed back her hair. What was the use of all
this grubbing toil?—in this never-ending turmoil that began
anew each day? What purpose could there be in a life that
held so little of joy and took that little away?

She stiffened, abruptly recalling Clem Andros' plight and
the note his messenger had lately brought. A covert glance
disclosed Krell's hard-faced deputies unsaddling. Her shoulders stirred impatiently. Her turning glance caught Flaurity
watching her; caught his odd, quick-masked expression. The
sound of Krell's laughter was still in her ears, and some reflection of its malevolence seemed to have lodged in Flaurity's
cheeks. Then he smiled a little, and there was in the curving
of his lips a gentleness and reassurance she had not seen there
before. Somehow this look of him helped her; she found it
good to know that here, at least, was one man she could de-
pend on. She thanked him with her eyes.

Her thoughts flew back to Andros who had such urgent
need of her, who was waiting out there somewhere cunning-
hidden in the hills—waiting in some brush-choked park or
canyon, hiding, hurt—sore in need of this food she had not
sent.. Needing a woman's care, perhaps!

She felt a renewed surge of fear. What if his messenger

no longer waited! What if he had gone and left the meeting place deserted without sign or indication of where she could find Andros!

The accelerated beating of her heart drummed one word frantically: Hurry! Hurry! Hurry!

But she must hide away from Flaurity the hurry she was in —the man had bade her gruffly leave Tom Flaurity out of this. Recalling words and look she almost doubted her new range boss; it were as though they did not trust him . . . But that was absurd! And yet—this man had come from Andros . . . She dared not risk it. She must get the food and go alone.

"Hurry! Hurry! Hurry!" an inner voice kept prompting. "Hurry ere it be too late!"

With impatient move of her shoulders she surveyed the yellow distance; her glance gone narrow, thoughtful. She remarked the depth and color of the stretching evening shadows; the afternoon was nearly gone. Another couple hours or so and night would send its curdling dark to hide this land away complete.

She said: "I think I'll ride," and started for the stable.

Flaurity demurred. "Better wait till after chuck. The boys'll be in—"

"Nonsense! I'll go—"

"Don't seem like you had ort to, ma'am," he argued, following. "Them two deputies Krell left won't be a heap in love with the notion. He put 'em here to watch us. Was they to see you streakin' off—"

He quit as she whirled angrily.

"Well," he shrugged, and said sarcastically: "I'm only the range boss round this place."

He saw at once how ill-timed was that reminder.

Flame's cheeks went gray and she swung lithe shoulders clear around and passed without an answering word inside the stable's doorway. She came out with her saddled horse.

Flaurity's eyes went bright and narrow.

Flame gripped the horn and with one cold look got grimly into the saddle. She whirled the bay, sent him drumming across the yard. The deputies shouted and, with a curse, caught up the gear they'd just stripped from their own broncs.

The bay took the Park trail going fast.

Andros' glance, from where he lay on the pine-slat bunk,

had fastened with a definite awareness upon the low-crowned hat of the smiling watcher. If he held scant knowledge of his whereabouts, at least he knew into what hands he'd fallen.

The man who lounged at smiling ease complacently eying him from the open door was the dreaded sheep king, Red Hat!

Red Hat grinned. "You're lookin' better. I thought you'd pull around."

Andros studied him with a taciturn interest. Talmage Vargas, he had heard, had started life under a Red River cart, and thereby learned at a tender age to make the most of everything. He was famous for the definite and unvarying order which he gave his men: "Feed my sheep!" He did not tell them how, nor little cared; he supplied them each with a pistol and a .30.30 rifle, and after that it was up to them.

This revealed the caliber of the man, his insight and his vision. He had learned the pitfalls of other sheepmen and shaped his plans accordingly. No plodding, stick-carrying walkers did their watching over Red Hat's flocks. He hired Chihuahua Mexicans, than whom there are no tougher breed; men who for long, lean years had labored in the yoke of rich hidalgos. He gave them modern weapons, good food and plenty of it, mounted them on swift and enduring horseflesh and did not scorn to toil beside them; and by these things discovered his *pelados* would cross any deadline cowmen set. Their years of slavery and hunger had shaped them well to Vargas' ends; their crowning desire was to kill someone and Vargas' plans gave them plenty of practise.

All this Clem Andros knew from hearsay and, seeing the man before him, believed it. There were no scruples on that dark face. Tall and spare was Talmage Vargas, a man of unpredictable actions, brash of opinion and ready always to fight or carouse at the drop of a hat or the bat of an eyelid. His creed was his own and he flaunted it openly. God, he said, grew grass for the sheepmen and cattle were run by weak-minded fools. The scraggle of beard on his hard, burnt face had never concealed the iron squareness of a jaw that heralded guts and stubborness. He had both; and his chin-strapped hat with its silver concho was symbol of the hardbitten trails his boots had traveled.

Vargas' gaze was long on Andros with a cool and careful probing.

Abruptly he roused and stepped inside. He rested his back

against a wall and from his vantage, with big thumbs hooked in cartridge belt, he chuckled softly. The sound was rich with a real, rare humor.

They were a lot alike, these two.

"So you're Clem Andros, black wolf of the wastelands. I've heard some about you these last few years."

"I've heard a few things of you," Andros said with a frosty twinkle aglint in his stare.

Vargas nodded. "So now vou're backin' these two-bit cow fools. For *what*, will you tell me? It's too damned bad. I could go a long ways with a ranny like you. . . ." He paused suggestively and Andros smiled.

But he made no answer. He had burned his bridges. Talk couldn't change it. Nor would Clem Andros if he had the chance.

The sheep king rubbed big shoulders against the wall and stood considering. After some time he said: "You're a fool to take chips in a game like this—to back that bunch of fourflushing nesters. Them cowmen ain't got an earthly chance. Even the cattle barons are backin' me! We got a pool. . . . You've mebbe heard of it?"

"I'm willin' to listen," said Andros grimly.

Vargas waved a hand. "No matter. There's big int'rests backin' us. We got this thing in a nutshell; these shoestring brush-poppers has got to go. Hell, it's progress, Clem—progress. You ought to see that—vou been around."

"I can see our oint all right."

" 'Course you can. Cattle have always lost to sheep—"

"I grant you that," drawled Andros smoothlv. "But this is another time, friend Talmage. Another deal. Things *do* change, you know; it's a part of that progress you been mentionin'."

Vargas' growl was harsh, intolerant. "Dont talk like a rattleweed-smokin' Hopi. If them crazy cow-prodders fight we'll give 'em another dose like Flowerpot. If they're smart they'll pull stakes an' drift. This 's day of the sheep. You can't git around it. These droughts have licked the cow crowd for us."

"Whv waste time retailin' that to me? I'm just a white chip in a no-limit game."

"You're that all right. You got a rep, too—for fightin'.

89

You couldn't hold out, but you could make this bloody. What's the use? Sheep'll win in the end anyhow—why go an' get yourself planted? These two-bit squirts in this Four Peaks country will bank on the luck of havin' you with 'em; they'll figure your guns to pull 'em through—*an' they can't!* You ought to know that, Andros. A lot of damn fools'll just get 'emselves killed an' you'll not have a goddam thing t' show for it when the fumes an' the gun stink blow away."

Andros with a somber gravity drawing its shadows across his cheeks thought it over, his mouth grim-etched, turning dour and moody. "The probabilities," he finally said, "sure camp on your words. There's a damn good chance you can cut the mustard. But there's one little item you're overlookin'. Most of these rannies you been callin' fools came into this country when it was a heap more wooly than you'll find it now. They were pioneers in the Salt River watershed. They fought the redskins for what they've got; they fought drought an' storm an' wind an' sun. They battled rustlers and range-hog ranchers. They've had plenty of practise; an' when a man fights for somethin', it gains in value. These small spreads ain't countin' their cattle in whopping herds. What little they've got thev've nursed along; but it's the land that's really got in their blood. That's somethin' for you to remember, Vargas. The land. It's a part of them—the part they'll die for."

Vargas snorted. "Sure they'll die for it—an' you along with 'em!" He brushed back his mop of red hair with an impatient gesture. "Quit bein' a fool!" he said exasperated. "I've put sheep in cattle country before. A lot of these nesters'll have to be killed—you're right about that; but it's been my experience the bulk of 'em'll roll their tails for other parts without ever waitin' to pop a cartridge. They may love their land but when it comes right down to the pinch they'll love their lives a whole heap better!"

"Then you're goin' through with it?"

Talmage Vargas laughed. "Did you reckon I was just cuttin' a rustv?"

"Well," Andros sighed, "I expect we understand each other. I'm no cut-an'-run hombre, neither." Relaxing on the bunk's pine slats he eyed the big sheepman somberly. "What was it you said about Flowerpot?"

Vargas chuckled. "It's been gutted, bucko. That's how much

good your called meetin' done you. The two hands was killed an' Teal himself has run off in the brush. That's just a sample to what we'll give 'em if you go on encouragin' these fools to fight."

Hard set and inscrutable were Andros' cheeks. He lay there eyeing the red-hatted sheepman with a dark smooth glance that gave away nothing.

Vargas said, "You're a large-bore gun, bucko. Plenty large. But one gun ain't enough, as you'll find. I've got this country good as licked right now."

"Time will tell."

Vargas grunted, swung away from the wall. But ere he could speak boots scuffed the planks of the open door's threshold. The man who came in loosed a sneering laugh. "Goin' to spend the whole day argyin'? Bash in his head an' be done with it! Hell's fire— *I'll* do it if you' gone chicken-hearted! I owe that bastard somethin' anyhow!"

Andros said to him, "That's right, Charlie. Why don't you try it?"

Grave Creek stiffened. "You think I couldn't?"

"Oh, I guess you're tough enough to kill a sick man—"

"Why, you—" Grave Creek snarled and his face went livid. He swelled and showed his raw cheeks bloated. He snatched out a gun and started for Andros.

"I'll handle this," drawled Red Hat coldly.

Grave Creek's swiveling eyes were like agate. "You been handlin' this for the past six days an' he's better now than he was when we found 'im! What game are you playin'? This skunk'll git the whole damn range—"

"What he gets is my business—an' the game is, too. You're just a cog in a big wheel, Charlie. You best keep it in mind," remarked Vargas softly.

There was in his glance some dim-seen thing that stopped Grave Creek where he stood and rooted him. The shadow he threw seemed someway shrunken. Color changed in his cheeks and to Andros it seemed that for all his talk this tall, chesty gun fighter was soft inside him, less sure of himself than he'd have men think—an intricate bit of oiled machinery over which dust had settled thickly.

Something then turned Andros' mind off Grave Creek Charlie with a clean abruptness. That unsent letter he had penned to Bocart was in his chaps pocket—torn up, but there to be pieced together and read if these fellows should happen to find it!

His narrowed stare raked Vargas' face. In that moment he almost groaned, for his wheeling glance failed to find his clothes on the floor by the table where he'd formerly seen them. If Red Hat got that letter——

God! Would he never do anything right in this business?

He said in a voice held coolly tranquil: "If you've got no objection I'll sit up for a spell; I'd like to get shut of this blasted dizziness——got to be gettin' my strength back sometime. My side's feelin' itchy so mebbe it's mendin'. Where'd you put my gear?"

"Never mind yore clothes," Grave Creek sneered. "You ain't goin' no place."

"No," grinned Red Hat. "No harm in your sittin' up though, if you want to. Wrap that blanket around you."

It would not do, Andros knew, to balk. He got shakily up on an elbow, paused there, resting, with sweat plainly shining across his forehead. He was not half as well as he'd hoped he was; but he swung his feet to the floor at last and pulled the blanket around his shoulders. He leaned back, closing his eyes, feigning a weakness far in excess of that he was feeling.

"I guess," Vargas said, "you'll not be needin' them duds for awhile."

Andros was thinking of that gleaming .30-30 leaned against the table. He kept his eyes shut for a good three minutes and hoped his face looked pale and drawn. He stared blearily round, trying to simulate the dizziness he had claimel to feel. If he could only get his hands on that yonder rifle . . .

Grave Creek stood curiously watching Vargas who was busily scribbling in a dog-eared tally book. At last Vargas stopped. His lips shaped a grin as he looked it over. He tore out the sheet, put the rest in his pocket. "I guess that'll do."

He looked at Andros. "Last chance, bucko. Throwin' in with me or ain't you?"

Andros didn't bother to answer.

With a snort the sheep king tossed the note to Grave Creek. "Have the cook take that to the Rockin' T. He's to give it to the Tarnell skirt—nobody else. Savvy? I want the girl to come back with him; tell him to read it an' use his head."

Grave Creek, reading, sniggered. "This'll bring 'er all right."

Vargas said, eyeing Andros: "Some gents take a lot of learnin'. I'm goin' to show you, bucko, that when Red Hat wants a thing, Red Hat gets it. Give him a peep at that note, Charlie."

Grave Creek moved to Andros' side. Still grinning, he held the note where Andros could read it. He did. He said to Vargas with curling lip, "You're wastin' time, Mister."

"We'll see."

"That thing won't fool—"

"It'll fool that Tarnell dame—wait an' see. It'll bring her out here quicker'n hell."

"She won't know who it's from—"

"Don't be so modest."

"She won't come, anyway. You've told her not to."

"You don't know much about women, do you?"

Dull color darkened Andros' neck. It took considerable to hold his temper. "You're overratin' her interest, Vargas."

The sheepman grinned. "I don't overrate things. She'll guess it's from you. She'll come out here, too."

"What good will it do you? I give you more sense than to try kidnappin' her, or holdin' her here against her will. What's the answer?"

But Vargas just grinned. "Give the cook the note," he told Grave Creek. "An' when you come back bring Andros' clothes. I kind of got a hankerin' to see what's in 'em."

12

THE CARDS ARE DEALT

FLAURITY knew the need of quick thinking.

Krell's deputies were plenty mad as they dashed for their horses. He didn't blame them much; he was peeved himself, her lighting out that way. There were several alternatives plainly before him. He did not cotton to any one of them.

He shrugged and spat and made after Krell's men.

"No sense gettin' all lathered up, gents. She's jest gone for a ride."

The biggest man swore. "I'll ride her when I get my hands on her!"

"Stow it," the other man growled peremptorily. He led his recaptured horse from the corral. "Slap on your saddle an' let's get goin'."

The big fellow growled but got to work.

"An' *you*," the short deputy said to Flaurity, "had damn' well better be round here when we git back!"

Then they were riding, ripping up the Park trail's yellow dust.

Flaurity waited till they'd gone from sight. He turned then and sprinted for the saddled bronc he had cached behind the foreman's shanty. He caught up the reins, lammed a boot in the stirrup. An instant later they were out of the yard, running hard toward the mountains.

Gallup John Murac, ex-marshal of Quinn River Crossing, made a rigid shadow against the rough adobe of his stable wall. He sat with both calloused hands in his lap and stared toward the wind-scarred front of the late Joce Latham's Golden Ox Saloon. He had held this posture for over an hour, with his hat pulled low to shade his eyes and his dark cheeks showing strictly enigmatic.

Sounds of argument, rising on the heated air, drifted to him from a dive across the road. Yet his face's grim contour showed no change; nor did it when, a little later, he saw Grace Latham leave the Golden Ox and, glancing quickly in either direction, move abruptly toward him. But his pulse stepped up as it always did when this girl came near, and there was a vast approval in the eyes that watched her clean-limbed stride.

She came into the stable and he rose to greet her. There was a heightened color in her cheeks that he knew came not from meeting him this way. Nor was it a thing of the hot sun's doing. Her searching scrutiny met his own gaze steadily.

"John." No hesitation marked her tone. "I've—" she said, and paused then plainly hard put to shape the rest of it. As she stood that way he read the diffidence in her bearing, the troubled light of her dark, level glance. "No," she said before he could speak. "I've no right to ask—"

"I told you once," he reminded gently, "to pass the word if you had any need of me."

"But this—"

94

"After all," he said, "I'm counted old enough to know my own mind."

They stood that way, silent for awhile, each busied with his own patterned thinking. He showed a faint touch of embarrassment beneath her long, continued scrutiny. He spoke with a voice that was not quite steady. "I—I'd do a lot for you, Grace."

A sharpness and a quick inquiry jumped into the glance she gave him. One hand came up a little uncertainly. Then she took the plunge.

"John— I've discovered where Andros has gone to!"

It was out. She stood there with her agitation evident; not noticing the deepened look of the lines about his firm-lipped mouth. Nor seeing the sudden stillness of his hands, or the hint of pallor raced across his cheeks. She was young and her mind was on her problem.

"There's a man inside the place—" Her shoulder gestured toward the Golden Ox. "A sheepman, I think. He's been talking with the barkeep, bragging. He's pretty drunk—been taking it on since noon. Red Hat's holding Andros prisoner! At the camp near Boulder Mountain!"

She moved a little nearer; said intensely: "John! We've got to do something—we've got to get him out of there!"

Gallup John got up. He stood there looking down at her, then sent his glance out across the range where it showed, framed dark, through the stable doorway. "Yes. I'll saddle up."

"I'm going too—"

"Better if you didn't, mebbe. I might have to unravel some lead."

"I'm going," she said; and followed him back toward the stalls.

The shadow of the tree trunk on the wall was three inches higher ere Grave Creek's returning boots crunched the gravel outside the door. He came in and tossed Red Hat a rolled-up bundle. "There's his clothes. The cook's on his way to the Tarnell place."

He leaned against the door jamb then, watching curiously as Vargas spread Andros' things on the floor and, squatting by them, began his search, systematic and careful.

Andros, looking ahead, could easy see where this was headed for. When Vargas found and repieced the fragments

95

of that letter to Bocart a crisis would be instantly at hand. In such an event his chance of continued life would be slight. If they did not kill him at once, the very least he could look forward to would be close watched incarceration till this question of National Forests was settled for once and for all.

It was in no way a pleasing prospect.

He said, "And where's my hat gone? What'd you do with it?"

"Forget it," grinned Grave Creek. "Where you're goin' they don't need hats."

"Don't be too sure of that," Andros countered. Hunched lower in his blanket he pulled its folds up about his chin.

Vargas frowned. "Go get the hat."

Reluctantly his gun fighter shoved free of the door jamb. He flashed Clem Andros a malevolent look.

Vargas called after him: "When you locate it bring it straight in. I'm doing the hunting." With a grin at Andros he picked up the chaps.

"I can't figure," Andros said, "what you think you're lookin' for. Don't seem like you could be so flat you'd take to robbin' a sick man's pockets. Sheep business must be lookin' mighty daunsy."

But Vargas, still with that faint half-grin, just grunted and kept on hunting. Seconds later his lips stretched wide in a saturnine smirk of triumph as he brought a handful of paper to light. Torn scraps, this was; the letter written by Andros in the hotel to Major Cass Bocart!

"The sheep business is lookin' up," Red Hat said with his grin turning sharp. His squatting figure bent a little forward then and he began ranging the bits of paper in a pattern on the floor.

Sunlight, slanting from the open door, shone full across the sheepman's face, making vivid each tough, a-grin angle, blocking out the square mass of his chin.

Swiftly, Andros knew, this crisis would be shaped for the payoff.

Hunched upon the hard pine bunk he considered this, briefly thinking back to other times when he had known this feel before. This was a little different though. The wound in his side, though nearly healed, was not without certain twinges of pain; and his faith in his abilities was not so great as it had been. He was weakened by the lack of food and the time he'd spent upon his back. These things were dead against him; but worst of all was the definite fact that he had no kind of weapon.

There was this one chance:

Vargas, intent upon his scraps of paper, was forward bent—to all appearances unmindful of him. Grave Creek Charlie was outside someplace, hunting the hat for Vargas.

The will to live was strong in Andros and in this fix, knowing Bocart's need and the trust the Major had placed in him, he would have taken chances greater than these. The need was urgent; it forced him to revalue the odds.

With glance hawk-bright on Vargas crouched in profile but five feet away, he got his legs beneath him and, snail-slow, lowered the blanket. He made no sound. But suddenly Vargas' head swung round. He was reaching for his hip when Andros sprang.

The encompassing hush of limitless space lay like the smash of sunlight all across the Half-Circle Arrow when Barstow opened the ranch house door to a frantic, hard-knuckled pounding. Immediately his burly shoulders tensed, and the voice that pushed his words out was a gutteral, rage-choked snarl. "What are *you* here for?"

Tom Flaurity said with an equal anger, "I've a hunch I'm bein' double-crossed! What was the idea sendin' Krell an' them damn' deputies—"

"Damn you!" Barstow shouted. "Have I got to take it up with *you* every time I make a move in this thing? If I'd got a man instead of a tinhorn to do the chore I give you, I'd of had no need for sendin' Krell! If you'd do your work an'—"

"I planted old Tarnell, didn't I?"

"An' was damn well paid for it, by God! Krell would of done that trick for less than half your price!"

"Tough you didn't think of him sooner!" Flaurity flared. "It's Krell this, an' Krell that till I hate the sound of the bastard's name! You must think a heap o' Flame Tarnell to be sendin' that damn stallion—"

"You shut your caterwaulin' mouth!" roared Barstow, starting for him with big fists clenched. "Another crack like that—"

"Take it easy, Barstow." Flaurity did not back a foot. "Lay paws on me an' I'll see a rope wrapped round yore windpipe,

97

bucko! What I know of your skunk tracks is plenty—savvy? An' I got it down in writin'."

Barstow paused in his forward reaching and with a bitter scowl put down his fists. "So you've got it down in writin', have you?" He stood there stiff, the bully cast of his big roan cheeks inscrutable. "So you've got it down in writin', eh?" His shoulders arched in a left-off shrug, and he swung them round as though to go back inside.

Flaurity's arm shot out to grab him back; and like that he was, with one arm reaching, when Barstow's burly shape came round with his teeth white-showing like a crack of light. One powerful fist smashed Flaurity's jaw with a sound that slapped clear across to the bunkhouse.

Flaurity dropped like a sack and lay loose-stretched on the yellow earth.

When, with a groan, he got one elbow finally under him, Barstow bent and yanked him up. He held him till he got his balance then shoved him at the waiting horse. "Git on that horse an' git back to your ranch, an' quick's you get there tend to that chore! You get him this time or I'll get *you!*"

13

"APOLOGIZE—AN' DO IT QUICK!"

EVEN as the force of Andros' hurtling body struck and smashed the sheep king backwards, Andros discovered what mistake he'd made in estimating Red Hat's character. Vargas was not slow; he was faster than chain lightning. He came up off the floor like a cat. One slashing fist smashed Andros sideways; a second, quick-following, struck his jaw. He lost his balance, crashed against the wall with both arms spread. But his waggling knees had no chance to drop him. Vargas' third blow did it for them. He went down the wall like a busted kite.

One folded knee struck braced and stopped him. He shook his head like a hammered bull and had barely clawed to a half-crouch, blear-eyed, when Vargas closed, intent on the kill. The pummeling of those rock-hard fists drove thought and all conscious action out of him.

The floor was dropping. He clutched at Vargas' middle and hooked clawed fingers in the sheepman's belt and clung there crazily while star after star exploded across the blackness of his mind.

Vargas, breaking the grip at last, backed off. On wabbling hands and knees Andros saw him as the only stationary thing in sight. With the punch fog and the roaring thinning Andros got a leg beneath him. He came upright without hearing any sound save the tempestuous pant of his own gasped breathing.

"You got enough?" said Vargas, grinning.

Andros watched him and could not control the trembling of his punished body. He found these moments of inaction precious. Standing off this sheepman was like tangling with a pile-driver.

But he would not quit.

Vargas saw that. "I'm goin' to put you back in bed, bucko. All set? You're askin' for this," he grunted. He closed in with his long back arched, putting his feet down like a cat.

Of a sudden he leaped with a slashing drive.

At the final moment Andros dropped his lean form slanchways and the sheepman's caroming body pitched over him, tripped upon that outstretched leg. Red Hat hit the wall with a force that shook the entire cabin.

Andros clawed unsteadily erect. He wheeled a whipped-out look at Vargas. But Red Hat lay unmoving. There was bright red blood in his tangled hair.

Andros' head throbbed madly from the punishment of Vargas' blows. He felt weak and sick and dizzy. There was a palsied shake in every limb. But he dared not waste a second. Where Grave Creek had gone he had no notion, but the man would not be away much longer. When he came back it behooved Clem Andros to be ready for him.

He caught up his trousers, pulled them on and buckled his chaps over them. He stamped into his boots while he buttoned the shirt across his chest.

He was reaching for Vargas' pistol when the scuff of boots crossed the boards outside. He dived for the gun. His fingers were just touching its grip when Grave Creek appeared in the doorway. Grave Creek yelled and slammed for leather.

Andros' spinning leap was lightning. Even as Grave Creek fired flame seared from Andros' pointing hand. One shot and, instantly, another pounded the room with sullen thunder.

99

Dust jumped from the front of Grave Creek's shirt. He staggered. One flailed arm tried to catch the doorframe, but it did no good. The hinges of his knees let go and spilled him backward down the steps.

He stayed where he stopped and did not move.

Andros drew a shaky breath. He came erect slowly. His cheeks and neck were agleam with sweat. All his muscles were slack and jerky. He quit looking at the man, wheeling to learn if Vargas had stirred.

Vargas had not. The blood was beginning to clot in his hair; aside from that there was no change apparent in the sheepman's posture.

For seconds longer Andros eyed him warily with eyes gone somber, the lines of his face completely grave. After which he turned away and rummaged the shack for his belt and guns. He found the belt and its scabbards but the pistols were gone. He ran over its cartridges quickly, then strapped it snugly round his waist and holstered Vargas' sixgun.

He stared once more at the shape on the steps. He could look back now and see that it had had to be this way; ever since that first encounter on Long Rope's street he had known sometime he would have to kill him. Grave Creek's injured vanity, his towering egotism would never have let it stop at less.

Andros wearily shook his head. The ways of a man caught up with him. Like Grave Creek he had lived too long by the gun to think different. Some place, some time, Black Andros too would meet a man whose hand was just that trifle faster —a man like Latham, but whose aim would be surer.

Well, so be it.

Then his shoulders stirred impatiently. He had better be getting out of this.

He picked up the .30-.30 that was on the floor by the table; cast a final glance at Vargas. The man was still out—probably would be for some time. He must have hit that wall with his head, Andros thought. But he would come to presently, or some one of his men would be along and find him.

It would not be good if he found Clem Andros.

Prudence counseled he tie the man, but he was too impatient to linger longer. Flame Tarnell was in his mind—and Red Hat's trickery. He must find her swiftly. Even now she might be riding —decoyed by the cook and that lying message.

100

The nails of Andros' clenched fists bit his palms. If she cared at all Flame would read that note as a challenge. Every instinct of her clean young life would be outraged by the picture painted by Red Hat's note. She would . . .

He closed his mind against that vision; and hurried out.

The sun smashed hotly across his shoulders—a blessed feeling to a man who for six long days, and six longer nights, had lain flat on his back, inactive, beneath a sheepman's blankets.

His side was sore and his bones ached badly, but his one concern was Flame Tarnell. He glanced at his shadow.

It was four o'clock.

This was enemy country. Red Hat's men must know he'd been prisoner; they would shoot on sight. An instinct—an overpowering need—of self-preservation warned him to be careful and he sent a long, probing look about him; at those ridges cutting the skyline yonder, at the brooding bulk that was Boulder Mountain, at the yellow earth and its seared new grass.

All the ways of his life had taught him caution; he stood awhile, stiff-placed, absorbed—gleaning impressions from the things he saw. There were many horse tracks on this ground; no sign of sheep. Bootprints were here in plenty with their heels deep-driven in the soft adobe. Some led toward a spring, others made a beaten path to the corral off yonder beside the alders.

There were broncs penned up in that pole enclosure. His own was there, but he dared not rope it out quite yet. Another cabin stood off to the left; there might be a man, or men, inside. He had to know. And he wanted one look for Bocart's pistol—the one Andros knew had belonged to Krell. If it was there to be found he'd no intention of leaving it.

The door was ajar. He shoved it inward with a kick of his boot and stood, gun drawn, awaiting action. But nothing happened. He stepped inside.

The shack was deserted. Cook shack, looked like. He looked round swiftly. Rusty stove. Rickety cupboard. Empty pail and unwashed dishes piled on a bench. Nothing here. Whoever had found him that night on the range had probably stolen the gun and slicker. He thrust a hand at hip pocket. They'd got his wallet, too.

He stared around outside for Vargas' and Grave Creek's horses; but he saw no saddled broncs in sight. Evidently they'd pulled off their gear and put the horses in the corral with the rest. There was a kak-pole yonder with three saddles on it. One was his own. He shouldered it, opened the corral gate. He dropped his hull, strode inside, shaking out a loop.

Six days of inaction had slowed his hand. He was awkward from the battering Red Hat's fists had given him. Accepting these facts, his face showed grim. Three minutes it had taken him to catch and saddle this pony. A man's ways caught up with him. . . .

He gathered the gelding's reins in left hand and reached for the horn—stopped taut as a bowstring. Rough wind shouldered across the flat, throwing its soughing through the needled pine branches. Faintly through it rolled the muffled drumming of distant hoof-beats. Loud, then soft, then loud again—coming nearer.

Two horses. They were running fast.

He waited no longer. He piled into the saddle and sent the gelding into a beaten trail that angled north-westward through the pine stand.

Flame Tarnell rode worriedly along the dipping, twisting humus-covered trail that swung its circle south of Boulder Mountain. Many times as she urged her horse after Andros' dour messenger her anxious eyes lifted to scan the four peaks that, yonder, darkly thrust themselves against the cloud-flecked sky. She was filled with a strange, oppressing restlessness; vague apprehensions that would not be shaken off.

She studied the night-blurred back of the man before her with a deepening curiosity. Strange messenger for Andros to have sent, she thought; but then recalled he had probably had no choice. The man had come within hailing distance of his hideout and Andros, knowing not when chance might bring another, had been forced to use him.

This was convincing logic, but someway it did not satisfy her.

The man ahead brusquely said, "Gettin' tired?"

"I'll make out."

He muttered something which the wind whipped away and a moment later increased the pace. They galloped steadily for twenty minutes. A fringe of trees loomed dark before them. She saw his hand raised through the murk and his horse slowed down, dropped back beside her. "We'll walk through this. You'll be talkin' with this guy pretty quick now."

She ought to feel glad, exultant, she thought. Her resentment of Andros' neglect had vanished when she read the note. He hadn't been able to get in touch with her. She understood his silence now.

Yet his messenger's words brought only dread.

She could not guess why this should be. Apprehension gnawed at her. Unaccountably she was filled with foreboding.

She tightened her grip of the reins and shivered. She slowed her horse until a larger interval stretched out between herself and the man ahead. For moments she lost sight of him. Then she rounded a bend in the tree-lined trail and found herself in a ghostly basin—a pocket whose pallid floor was studded with the red-tipped wands of ocatilla. Her escort was waiting by a Joshua tree.

He said: "Stick close—we turn here. The trail's—"

She said, "This looks like Ballantine Can—"

He cut her off with a heightened curtness. "We ain't takin' the Ballantine trail." He turned his horse. "Come on," he said.

"Are you heading for Little Pine Flat?"

That wheeled him square around in the saddle. "Bring that horse up closer."

She kneed her horse. The man's hand shot out and caught its cheek strap. The animal snorted—danced three sideward steps. He forced it round till its saddle was beside his own. His beard-stubbled face showed with greater clarity. She saw the gleam in his narrowed, squinting stare.

"Yes?" Only her will kept that single word free of tremor.

"I'll take yo' gun," he said; and before she could move to stop him he had lifted the pistol out of her holster. Then he settled back, thrusting the weapon inside the waistband of his trousers. "Y'u'll be able to keep up better now, I reckon. Ride a lot lighter without that hogleg."

With deadly calm she asked, "What was your idea in doing that? Am I a prisoner—"

"If y'u are," he jeered, "y'u've got no kick. I told y'u plenty that y'u wasn't wanted—but y'u *would* come."

Flame drew one quick, taut breath and stared at him.

The man laughed. "No sense gettin' riled. Y'u're here now —better make the best of it. Yo' been cravin' to see that fella,

103

an'y'u're goin' to. We've got him holed up in Red Hat's sheep camp."

He chuckled smugly. "Andros said that note wouldn't fetch y'u. Red Hat knowed——"

He swayed in the saddle, wildly clutched for the horn as Flame's spurred horse drove into his own. Flame's slashing quirt cut whistling sound that stopped at his face. He cringed, wild, swearing. Then swore again—ripped the quirt from her hand. "By Gawd," he snarled, "I'll learn y'u somethin'!"

He was grabbing a violent hold on her when a cold, flat voice said:

"Apologize—*an' do it quick!*"

14

THE BOARDS OF A CABIN FLOOR

FLAME felt Andros' messenger stiffen. Through the ghostly gloom she saw the rolling whites of his startled eyes—saw the livid marks of her quirt on his cheek. His insucked breath was a chill-clawed sound. He let her go with a hoarse-snarled oath and rocked back into his saddle with his right hand streaking hipward.

"If you're faster than Grave Creek keep on reachin'."

Flame Tarnell hysterically stifled an impulse toward laughter. The stiffness of the man's stopped shape was ludicrous. She watched him slowly turn in his saddle, slit eyes peering for the speaker's shape.

She knew that voice—it belonged to Andros. She could see that this man, too, suspected it. His edgy turning showed a visible caution. His eyes were stretched wide and his face was chalky.

A wild exultation rushed through Flame. It crammed her lungs and threatened to stifle her; but she was *glad, glad, glad!* She knew a mighty joy. Black Andros was free and very much alive; and all the world was filled with glory!

Cold fear blanched the cheeks of the man before her. If there was glory about him he saw no part of it. He cringed like a dog and his hands were shaking. Flame reveled in the

104

knowledge. Black Andros had a way this man could understand!

She did not turn to seek Andros out; she watched the pseudo guide with an alive, malicious interest. She would not let Andros shoot him, but she meant him to think Andros would to the last. It was a fate he richly deserved and had merited.

No motion swayed the man's stiff shape. His hand still hung where it had stopped by his belt. His upper body was forward crouched and his frightened gaze watched Andros fixedly.

"I'm still waitin' for that apology, mister."

"I—I'm sure beggin' the lady's pardon—"

"For decoyin' her out here?"

"For decoyin' her out here—"

"An' for takin' her gun?"

"An' for takin' her gun—"

"An' particular for what you was just fixin' to do?"

"Yeah. F-For what I w-was fixin' to do—*Gawd, yes!*"

"That satisfactory, ma'am?"

Flame nodded, too filled with the tumult of this thing and of her thoughts to speak.

But Andros seemed to understand.

"All right, friend. Drop that gun," he ordered; and a feel of change lashed across the gloom.

The man licked dry lips. His eyes jerked round in searching stabs that seemed to hunt for some way out. All the brashness seemed drained out of him. He was filled with desperation.

The night, Flame thought, seemed abruptly colder. She wondered what things the treacherous messenger read in Clem Andros' look. She watched him gingerly take the gun from his holster.

"Throw it into that pear thicket," Andros bade quietly.

The man's hesitation was plainly apparent. Flame guessed how much he wanted to turn the pistol in his hand till its muzzle eyed Andros. But he didn't dare. With a raking groan he tossed it from him.

Flame looked at Andros then.

He stood so near she could almost have touched him. He stood tipped a little forward. His haggard cheeks showed no emotion. But his gaze was smokily hot and bitter and all his weight seemed to rest on the balls of his feet.

105

"Climb off that horse."

Awkwardly the man obeyed. He stood beside the pony nervously, tight of lip and watchful. Slow lights burned in his glinting stare.

"What y'u fixin' t' do?" he blurted.

"What do you think I'd ought to do?"

The man had no answer for that. Flame saw him tremble.

"I'm goin' to send you back to Vargas," Andros told him. "You seem pretty handy at deliverin' messages. Tell Red Hat this: No sheep will cross the Four Peaks range. Get goin'."

It was not till Flame saw the sheepman turning that she remembered he still had the pistol he'd taken away from her. It was too late then—*his shoulders were swinging in a vicious arc.*

Her scream and the shot rang out together.

It was Andros' gun that threw the flash; she saw the glint of his teeth in the gun's explosion.

The little man staggered. He reeled three steps and hung there, swaying. He was trying to speak but no words came though the groan welled out of him. And suddenly he was down, a dark still shape beneath the Joshua.

Flame felt the tug of Andros' glance but she would not look at him. Deliberately she turned her back on him.

His voice reached out gruffly. "What's wrong? Good Lord! You don't think I engineered that, do you?"

Flame said stiffly: "Yes. That's exactly what I think!"

He said impatiently, "Don't be a fool!" and she heard him coming toward her.

She could have hugged him three minutes sooner. Now she was coldly furious, convinced it had been his intention all along to kill the man. She said, bitterly resentful, "Don't come near me!" and turned her face to show him her opinion of a man who would do the contemptuous thing she believed Black Andros had done.

"I've no intention of coming near you," he said; and whirling, she saw that he was approaching the dead man's horse.

His lifted glance regarded her gravely. "You can start on back. I'll be right with you. I think that fellow has my slicker. By the look of them clouds I'd say you'll be needin' it pronto."

She answered icily: "I've one of my own, thank you." But this time, despite the scorn of her tone, she did not turn away. Curiosity compelled her to watch his movements.

Her glance stayed on him while he unfolded the slicker behind the dead man's cantle, while he shook it out and examined it. She caught the slight compression of his lips, so close was her own horse to him.

Andros, after looking it over, draped the slicker across an arm and bent above the dead man's side. Presently he rose and Flame could see the glint of something in his hand. She saw him fling the thing aside with an impatient gesture and at once make off toward the pear clump into which the pseudo guide had flung his pistol.

A little grimly she wondered if he were not touched, or something. It would, she thought, be fitting retribution. Why should he be poking into the thorny maze of that prickly pear? Was he hunting for the dead man's gun?

Apparently, he was, for a moment later she saw him straighten with it. She heard his grunt and wondered why he should be staring off into the night with that painfully hunted pistol unregarded in his hand.

Andros wheeled with an impatient lift of his shoulders and came striding back to the dead man's horse. He stood still before it, then caught up its reins and looped them about the saddle horn. Stepping back he slapped the animal smartly, watching as it moved off down the basin.

He put the slicker on and gave a peculiar whistle. His horse loomed in the yonder darkness and came trotting up like a well-trained dog. Stiffly Andros climbed aboard.

"All right," he said.

"Aren't you taking a lot for granted?"

He stared sharply at her, shrugged and swung his pony's head to the backtrail. "Look," he said. "I'm not likin' this any more than you are. But when a chore's to be done there has to be some ranny game to do it. I told you that when I took this job. I said no halfway stuff would cut it."

He regarded her morosely, parallel wrinkles upsetting the smooth pallor of his forehead. "I told you right at the start you'd have to trust my judgment—I said there'd be times when you wouldn't be likin' it none. This is one of them times. I got to play this as I see it. I guess I'm stubborn; but when I take on a job of work I rattle till it's finished."

"Was Joce Latham's woman a job of work?"

She saw the color that bit his cheeks, but his words were

smooth enough. He said, "I guess there's some would call her one." Then, harsh, intolerant, he growled: "Mind tellin' me the name of the polecat that's been packin' tales—"

"I certainly do. I'll not have any more murders on my conscience—"

"So you've got a conscience, have you? I been entertainin' some doubts of it." His glance stabbed across at her darkly. "Let's get this straight. I went into town on business. Joce Latham jumped me and I—" The pause was slight, but it was there. He finished doggedly: "I had to kill him. Leavin' town I was feelin' kind of weak I guess—"

"I don't believe I'm interested," Flame said with lifted chin. "I expect Joce Latham's woman would find—"

"Yes," he said, "I expect she would." Then, savagely: "What do you take me for? You ought to know I've been held prisoner. By Red Hat's crowd. That note—"

"Oh! So you sent that note to me, after all! I might have—"

"If you think I wrote that note—"

"I *know* you wrote it! You proved it when you killed your messenger! You were scared the man might tell me!"

Incredulity was in Andros' look. His gaunt face went suddenly dark. "Okay," he said, "I sent the note. Where do we go from there?"

Flame said, "I'm going *home;* where you go doesn't interest me."

"That's good. I'll trail along then."

Flame wheeled her horse in bitter wrath. "You'd better go back to Latham's woman—you seem to understand her kind."

"I can see I'll never understand *yours!*" Andros said.

They sat their saddles, resentment like a blade between them.

Andros said with a lift of his shoulders: "Probably just as well, at that. A hired hand's got no time to waste thinkin' about his boss—"

"You're not wasting any time of mine. Your name came off my payroll the day you rode in to see Grace Latham—Tom Flaurity's giving the orders at Rockin T these days."

"You seem to have already forgot one of the main things I been tellin' you. I'm the kind of guy that sticks. When I hire on I don't get shucked till all the steers been counted. You can put Flaurity back in the bunkhouse. Or," he finished maliciously, "I'll put him back myself."

He heard the sharp intake of her breath. If she'd had her quirt she'd have struck him sure. "You *gun fighter!* I'm sorry I ever crossed your trail—"

"No sorrier than me," he growled. "You'll have reason to thank your stars I *am* a gun fighter before this thing is finished." He took his resentful look at her. "If you're all through pouring in the broadsides now I expect we better get along. Happens in my hurry gettin' shut of Red Hat's camp I forgot to loose the remuda. So if you ain't hankerin' to see me carve another three-four notches on my guns you better start layin' tracks."

They were near to gunshot of the Rocking T, still riding in the grip of turbulent thoughts, when the first big flattened drops struck down, lashing up the yellow dust, creating sullen mutter in the dim-seen tracery of hemming trees. Flame did not make of this rain an excuse for speech. Clem Andros rode in a black, tight quiet that proclaimed if any talk were started she'd be the one to do it.

Wet horse smell was in his nostrils and the legs of his pants were soaking water where the drip ran off his chaps; but he would not break this riding silence if he never talked again. The things she'd said still rankled, still raked him with their unjust spurs. There was no understanding a woman—the sex was hell any way you took it!

That was a good enough conclusion; but getting Flame out of mind was something else again. It amazed and shamed him to find what hold she still had on his thoughts. He felt meeching as a yellow hound to think he could still feel interest in a girl who had used him so. What kind of pelican was he that his pride could stoop to such admittance? Did girls affect all men like this? A sorry world if it were so!

His bitter glance took in the slicker-covered shape of her; and he went suddenly stiff in the saddle. The recollection that had come to stop him that way in his tracks was staggering. *That note to Bocart!* The torn scraps of it were still where the fight had left them—littering the boards of the cabin floor!

15

LOW EBB

IT WAS after midnight when the girl and Andros came in sight of the Rocking T. The house was dark, but from the foreman's shanty a light gleamed pale and mistily through the curtain of rain.

"Might's well settle this right now," Andros told himself, and sent his horse across the sloshy yard. He stopped it in the veranda's gloom, swinging down, aware that Flame was wheeling after him.

He strode beneath the dripping eaves, boots squelching on the spongy gumbo, and stepped upon the porch's wet planking. There was measurement of his temper in the way one booted foot sent the shut door banging open.

The place was empty. There were crumbs and an unwashed cup on the table. The coffee pot still held its warmth.

It reminded him of his search for Krell. This was the way it had always been; never once had he come upon a place with Krell still there. Many times he had missed him by this fraction.

Now he was missing Flaurity. There was irony in it for him.

His wheeling shoulders put him face to face with Flame. There was something odd, he thought, in her glance. "So he isn't here," she said, and he'd have sworn that she breathed easier. What had she been afraid of? That he would kill the man? Yes; that was it.

Under his close look her wet cheeks took on color. Resentment raised her chin, and he read nervousness into the gesture with which she pushed the damp hair from her eyes.

He wiped the water off his nose, took off his hat and shook it. This girl's attraction hit him hard. He had to fight it, for her nearness was an unsettling thing. It had the power to make him forget his rancor; it dug up hungers he hadn't known were in him.

She said, "I guess you'll know me next time."

"Did you think I'd ever forget you?" The words came

110

roughly. Emotion shoved him toward her; and she looked up with a catch of breath when, close, his arms closed round her, crushed her close against him. The wild fragrance of this nearness was too much and he kissed her savagely, exultantly, wild tumult slogging his arteries.

He let her go abuptly, stepping back and suddenly conscious she had offered no resistance. His nerves tingled in this brittle silence; but there was nowhere in him any least regret. He said gustily: "I reckon you won't be forgettin' me, either—"

Her eyes were bright as diamonds. She said, "You *fool!*" and drew a tremulous breath. "Get off this ranch and don't come back here ever!"

The cynical curl of his lean wide lips was the only answer Black Andros made. He went past her through the door and crossed the dark veranda to his horse. He came back with a .30-.30. "See this?" He slapped the dark blue barrel. "You've given out you'll fight if Red Hat's sheep come back. This is Red Hat's answer." He slapped the gun again and said, "You're goin' to find out how they put Old Home Week on in hell. Them Chihuahua gunslicks he's imported—"

She said, "I'm not interes—"

"You better *get* interested! You made your brag you'd fight an' I've played the hand accordin'." His grin was cold and sudden. "You're goin' to fight an' like it!"

"All right, I'll fight—but I don't need any help of yours!"

"You're gettin' it anyway. I told you I was the kind that sticks—"

"Yes. When it comes to forcing unwanted attentions on women you shine with real determination."

The rise and fall of Andros' breathing was the only sign of movement in him. He stood there silent, somberly watching the play of light across her scornful features and wondering how a room could get so cold so quickly.

Fatigue etched heavy lines beneath his bloodshot eyes and brought up in dark shadows across the hollows of his cheeks. A slogging bitterness was in his stare.

He squared his shoulders then. "I'm stickin' anyhow," he said, and wheeled his silver spurs around her to stop suddenly in the doorway, listening, his glance gone into the night with cat-quick vigilance.

But all Flame heard was the purr of rain on the roof overhead. It obtruded on the restless quiet, lifting its sullen mumble to a full attack upon the puddled yard, then dropping to a duller mutter through which at last she heard the pound of hoofs.

A cold wind ran the valley. The slogging hoof sound rose in volume. Premonition touched the girl with icy fingers. Where were the sheriff's deputies? Was this the sound of their returning? Where had Flaurity gone to?

Her glance at Andros was sharp with worry.

Time crawled, and through the rain the hoof sound crept ever nearer and nearer.

Andros' grunt was a plain command. "Douse that light an' close the door."

She killed the lamp and stood there looking to where his lean form made a dark, crouched shape against the night's drenched black. It seemed aeons before her straining eyes picked out the blur of advancing horsemen. They had slowed to a walk; the reach of their wind-driven voices was sharp and harsh with anger. They were arguing. One—she believed it the voice of the biggest deputy—growled: "Don't I know a light when I see one?" Another voice snarled, "Where the hell is it now then?"

Then the horses stopped. Some vagary of the wind now dropped the riders' tones to an incomprehensible muttering. Flame said to Andros softly: "You better sharpen up your gun-cutting knife—there's two more notches waiting out there," and was instantly sorry.

Andros' voice ran the murk with a reckless temper. "That's far enough. Sing out your handles—quick!"

She saw then that, dismounted, the deputies had been sneaking forward. They were under thirty feet from the foreman's shanty when Andros' shout sailed out and stopped them. They crouched in the rain-soaked gloom and seemed to be peering round them uneasily. Then one of them growled: "Who's talkin'?"

"I'm wantin' those handles," Andros said. "I'm countin' three—"

"Shane an' Hodders. Deputy sheriffs."

"Deputies, eh? What are you doin' out here?"

"Sheriff's orders. We got word this crowd was— Say! You ain't seen that female, hev you?"

112

Andros' voice was grim and earnest. "Climb back into them saddles—"

"What for? We spent half the goddam night—"

"You leavin'?"

"No. By Gawd—"

From the veranda's edge a streak of flame bit wickedly into the rain-soaked dark. Echoes flattened against the buildings hemming the yard. A curse, a squeal and the sloshing splut of sprinting boots swift rose to mingle with the startled snorts of the frightened broncs.

The men had plainly reached their saddles. The big deputy's sulphurous tones sailed back in muttered threats. Once again Andros' lifted rifle put muzzle light across the dark and retreating hoof sound slapped the night. Andros sent his shout ringing after it. "Tell your boss this spread ain't needin' his advice. Next one of you I catch round here will be needin' a coffin though—remember it!"

Andros tried another match to the limp cigarette that hung from his lips and, swearing softly, dropped them both and ground a boot heel on them. A good two hours had passed since Flame had stormed from this cabin, yet Andros' jaw still showed its stubborn angle. The breach between them had grown beyond repair, and it were better so. He could put his mind to the business now. He'd been telling himself that for the last two hours but his mind didn't seem to hear him. It took note, though, of the sudden draft that struck across his neck.

Cat-quick he slewed around to find the door wide open.

Framed against the slanting rain big Flaurity stood with his shoulders pushed grotesquely forward. Water dripped from his sodden coat and he was breathing heavily. Maliciousness was bright in his stare. He said, "You're goin' to stay here *this* time!"

16

TEMPER

ANDROS' muscles cocked themselves.

Tom Flaurity was on the edge of murder!

Fact and purpose were shouted from a thousand details; that curious posture and balefulness of feature, his parfleche-taut skin, the white-knuckled tenseness of his widespread hands and the undulant flame that redly flared in the vacuous eyes watching Andros. Far too long had Black Clem probed life's hazards and conned the obscure shifts of men to be mistaken now.

Flaurity aimed to kill him, to gun him in cold blood.

Andros sat with twisted torso, held rigid by the knowledge that his slightest move would be, to Flaurity, the signal for unraveling lead. Flaurity's placement had him at a wicked disadvantage. He had turned in his chair at the feel of that damp air, wheeling his head and upper chest to get this look at Flaurity, and so had brought his hands to the left. He wasn't wearing his own two guns, for Red Hat's crowd had taken them. He was packing Red Hat's pistol, and it was holstered on the right. Might as well have been in Frisco for all the good it was like to do him. And besides all this he was still in the chair.

Every twisted nerve yelled protest. But he dared not move.

Rain beat loud on the yard and roof.

He shoved blunt words at Flaurity; sharp breathing packed the words with hurry. "What you doin' here? Where are the men? Where the hell has Red Hat got to? Speak man—don't stand gapin'! Speak up quick!"

The questions pummeled Flaurity like the blows of a blunted crowbar. You could sense the urgency of them battering at his consciousness—could feel them skidding across the armor of his fixed desire.

The copper of his gaze was curdling.

Andros followed his advantage, swearing like a man bad

114

used. "Damn you, Tom—speak up! Where are those blasted deputies? *You get Latham's note?*"

That last was a touch of genius, for Latham, of course, was dead. But Andros was shouting anything that came to mind; caring little what it was or that it made any sense at all, so it tangled Flaurity in the maze of his slow reactions.

And it worked!

Flaurity's jaw fell open and his eyes showed a stunned bewilderment. Andros jumped to his feet still cursing; and Flaurity, on the defensive and wondering where and how he'd erred, clean lost his advantage and never knew it till, suddenly, Andros grinned.

Andros said, "When you aim to gut a man, do it quick an' get it over—don't stand around swallerin' hogwash."

Flaurity got it, then. His head jerked down and he hit a crouch, and the fingers of his right hand spread; and color spread up from his neck, making wicked stain on his wax-pale cheeks.

"Your chance has went," drawled Andros. "You ain't got nothing but a busted flush."

The gnawing agony of choice put twitching lines in Flaurity's face. But he had guts. He said: *"We'll see!"*—and lost his nerve on the instant, for there was Black Andros, gun in hand, with his pistol's muzzle aimed dead center on the dripping third button of Flaurity's coat.

Andros' laugh was softly mocking. Then brashly, recklessly, he twirled his gun by the trigger guard and dropped it back in leather. "Go on," he murmured—"shuck 'em!"

To Flaurity his look seemed cold as ice. He could feel its chill in his own veins, freezing. Short moments gone he had entertained notions—violent and bloodthirsty purpose. He had meant to murder Andros where the fool had sat with his back to the door. That had been his fatal mistake; he should have done it from the rain-drenched darkness of the puddled yard.

The will to murder was in him still, but something balked the nerves of his hands; they would not do what his brain commanded. Desperation's courage had brought him to the brink, but it could not take him over. That bravery was gone, suddenly and completely whelmed in the sweat that bathed his back.

He stood stiff legged and forward tilted—rooted. He could

no more have dragged the heavy gun that sagged his belt than he could have flown. Fear—cold fear had clutched his muscles.

The girl, pistol in hand, peering white-faced through the shack's side window, could see no menace in Andros' pose; it was, in her eyes, the epitome of studied carelessness.

But she was not looking into Andros' eyes. She could not see that rising, falling, wanton flame that was defying, taunting, daring big Flaurity to touch his gun's wet handle.

Flaurity knew himself outsmarted. Andros was not bluffing now. He had it this time, cards and spades.

Spades! The thought made Flaurity cringe.

He writhed at the ease with which this grinning outlander had turned the tables, depriving him of his sure-thing edge. He had thrown the game away by striving to make sense of foolish words that had none.

Cursing himself for that folly he shivered to think of facing Barstow with this tale—then abruptly realized the scant likelihood of ever having again to face Reb Barstow with anything. He roused from his abysmal dread to find Andros plying him again with questions. He stared at the outlander sullenly. A crick in his back ached viciously, but he dared not mend his posture. He hardly dared even draw his breath. And then—but no! He could not believe it! A trick! A sneaking, scurvy, tinhorn trick! A ruse designed to trap him! But he could not choke his quick words back. *"What's that?"*

"Said you better talk fast if you're aimin' to get out of here whole."

It was the first token Flaurity had that Andros might be disposed to let him off without reprisal. Reaction hit him like a backhand blow; relief came near unhinging him. He reached a shaking hand to the doorframe; sagged against it weakly.

He licked dry lips. "A-Ask again—ask that over, will you?"

"Who told the sheep crowd I was callin' a meeting?"

"Not me—not *me!* I'll swear it wasn't me! I—"

"Did you tell Barstow?"

Flaurity hesitated. He darted anxious glances round, but found no comfort. There was no assurance any place. "What was—"

"You heard me. Come on—get at it."

116

Flaurity's glance licked round again. It brought up suddenly, shocked, at the window. He'd seen a white face briefly there—the steely glint of a pistol's barrel.

It left him limp. New sweat stood out on his forehead. Stiff-lipped he whispered, "I—I told him . . . yeah."

Andros' glance got keen and searching. "It was Barstow got you on here, wasn't it? How'd he work it? What'd he tell old Tarnell about you?"

The words came like the stab of a knife. They bugged Flaurity's eyes with terror. Dread closed like a rope about his throat. Too clear he saw where this trail led.

His nerves were scraped too raw for craft. He stared at Andros numbly.

"Come on—I want the truth."

But softness was a mask with Andros; it could not deceive Flaurity further. The glove was off, the hand revealed. Flaurity tore the collar of his shirt open, panting. He could not get rope's feel from his neck. He cringed away from Andros' stare.

Andros dropped a hand to his holstered pistol. "The choice," he said with summer's mildness, "is entirely yours, Mister Flaurity."

Flaurity broke.

Contempt curled Andros' lips. It was not a pretty thing he saw.

"Come! Get it over, man! Barstow got you this job here. He was pretty thick with Tarnell them days. He wanted Tarnell out of the way—"

"I didn't savvy that till later. He said—"

"I don't give a damn what he said! The truth is what I want from you, Flaurity. Regardless of the details, you killed Flame's father—"

"It's a lie. I never!" cried Flaurity hoarsely. "Swear to *Gawd* I didn't!" His face was like a gaub of putty. "It was Dakota!" he whined desperately. "Dakota—I can *prove* it was Da—"

"Don't bother."

An odd look showed in Andros' stare. It went through and beyond big Flaurity; it was as though the man weren't there. And Andros' voice was even more strange. "Get aboard your bronc an' make tracks—far apart ones that'll take you places. Don't linger an' don't stop."

Like a whipped cur Flaurity left.

Long moments after the last dim echo of Flaurity's leaving had been drowned in the slogging rain, Black Andros stood there, chin on chest.

But presently he roused and set about the cleaning of the gun he'd taken from Red Hat's holster. He got a box of cartridges from the cupboard and filled the loops of his gun belt. An edgy restiveness marked all his movements.

"Dakota, eh? So Barstow's got a Dakota on his payroll. And Bocart had a Dakota's sixgun. Hmm . . . Dakota. I expect we better see," he murmured, and slid broad shoulders into his slicker. He pulled the brim of his soggy hat down low across his eyes and stepped through the open doorway, so full of what he was thinking as to be oblivious to the danger of that lamplight back of him.

At veranda's edge he paused, confronted by an unexpected figure. "What you doin' out here in the rain?"

It was Flame Tarnell. He could see her shiver. By the refracted glow from the shack's lit lamp he could see how pale, how drawn was her look. There were circles under her eyes, dark smudges; and her glance was strange—oddly different. He could feel the shake of her hand on his arm.

"Clem . . ." Her voice was husky. "Let's be friends again."

He stared at her sharply. She seemed to mean it. For that one instant exultation gripped him. He forgot all rancor—his just resentment; remembering only the wild warm feel of her lips against his.

She said, "Let's put away our differences; the mean things we've said. Let's go back to where we left off the night we met."

The thrill of remembrance fell away from him. This was his curse—this need for detail that must ever probe beyond spoken words for the thing that was back of them, the motive or impulse that gave them birth. He paused, considering; and shook his head.

"It's a little late for that."

"But Clem—"

"A man can't go back. He can only go forward—or stand still and rot."

Wheeling, he reached for his saddle.

"Where are you going?"

Her sharp words swung him round. He said bleakly, "I'm takin' care of a chore—"

"You're going to Barstow's!"

"You called the turn. What—"

"But you *can't!* I won't let you! I heard what Flaurity told you and—"

"Eavesdropper, eh?"

He caught the flash of her eyes—her wild anger. "I own this spread and I've a right to know what's going on!"

"You know now."

"No thanks to you!"

"I want no thanks." Again he turned, reaching up for the saddle; but she whirled him round.

"Aren't you satisfied? Haven't you done enough? You can't believe those lies about Barstow— Surely you . . . Why, he's all I've left to turn to!—the one person who's stood by me from the start. If you hadn't come that night and got me all stirred up with your talk about his help I'd be married to him now—"

"An' still regrettin' it, like enough. The man's a crook," said Andros bluntly. "Why don't you quit this damn play-actin' an' face the facts He's thrown over all his small-fry friends; he's playin' in a big game now—playin' to win. I'll give him benefit of doubt—say he was an up-an'-comin' square-shooter once. But he's a hell of a long way from bein' one now! A gila monster could waddle right over him an' never touch! He's got one virtue—the determination of a mule. That's the most I can say for him."

"Do you always talk about people who are not around?"

"Call this a rehearsal; I'll tell him to his face. The man's rotten to the core! Why d'you suppose the sheepmen have kept their woollies off his grass? Because they're 'fraid of him?—because he's got more hands than you? Don't make me laugh! It's because he's a part of the Pool—that's why! The politics pool; the Big Interests' pool. The sheepmen, lumbermen, railroads an' big cattle barons that want to spike the Salt River watershed—the crowd that's fighting the National Forests! Barstow's the cattle kings' rep in that bunch!"

She didn't believe him; and said so, hotly. Her blue eyes flashed and she said: "I don't believe a word of it!"

"How much of this range do you own?" he said grimly.

119

"Two or three hundred acres—"

"Patented? Got title to it?"

"Certainly."

"How much range do you normally run on?"

"Ten or twelve miles, I suppose, most generally—"

"But you've got title to around three hundred acres? All right," Andros said, "I'm going to tell you somethin'. Your fine Reb Barstow's after that title."

The brittle sound of her laugh was derisive. "Are you *crazy?* Reb's got more range than he can use right now—"

"Right now, mebbe. But it's the title he's after. Else why would he be in such a sweat to get married? Didn't he go stormin' off like a wet potato when you wouldn't up and marry him—"

"I don't care to discuss that," she said disdainfully. "Your manners—"

"Manners be damned!" Andros flashed, and stopped. Flame looked as though she were going to slap him. "Go on," he said. "Mebbe it'll make you feel better. Has your fine friend been around since?"

She wheeled away from him—but not before he had seen his answer. "I see he ain't," he said, darkly satisfied.

She came square around. "He's been here twice!"

"Fine! But he came to do some more arguin'."

He could see by her face that Barstow had. He said, "I guess I better tell you a few. 'Twouldn't be brotherly to let you tie up to that kind of lobo without—"

"I won't listen to your vicious lies—"

"I'll tell 'em anyway." There was a stubborn jut to Andros' jaw. "Ordinarily I ain't much of a hand for—"

"Don't you think," she threw her protest at him, "I'm old enough to judge for myself what is best for myself?"

He didn't; but he was beginning to realize argument was useless. He eyed her dourly. With a shrug he sighed. "All right. Go ahead. It's not my funeral. If you're bound an' determined to ruin your life—"

He stopped when he saw the curl of her lips. He stopped and stood there irresolute, thinking back to the night of their fateful meeting. Much had happened in the time since sped, but little of aid to the small rancher's cause, and nothing at all toward the winding up of the chore Bocart had set him.

120

And there was that cursed note that he'd left in the cabin; Vargas, ere now, would have patched it and read it.

His shoulders stirred and changed thinking ran its darker shades across his cheekbones. His lifted glance caught Flame's regard. She was stepping closer with one hand toward him and lamp's light bright on her rain-wet face.

"Is fighting Reb really necessary, Clem? Can't you find some other way—"

He said morosely, "I told you once. I'll do what I have to do—hell or high water."

"Are you sure it isn't just plain, mean spite?"

"Spite!" He laughed shortly. "I've got no spite against Barstow. He's swimmin' in water that's over his head. I'm goin' to warn him out while he still can get out."

"You're sure it's not just me that moves you?"

"You don't enter into it, Flame. You cut no ice one way or the other."

It was Andros' unhappy faculty to rub her ever the wrong, rough way. And her pride was strong—as strong as his. But she humbled it. "Clem, leave Barstow out of this. For my sake, let it drop."

"You think a heap of that bull-headed Dutchman, don't you?"

So careless he was with his words—so roughshod. So blind he could be in the grip of temper.

She pulled her chin up, bitterly watching him. "Will you?"

"No!" he said curtly; swung up in his saddle.

Her voice was a whisper, but strong to reach him. "You better take the advice you left Flaurity. Don't come back. There'll be nothing for you here."

He showed her a twisted smile.

"At least," he said, "there'll be men to kill."

17

JOLT

A LUMPY COUCH draped with a faded blanket was shoved against one wall of Barstow's ranch office. He was seated on it, scowling. A contributing cause to his ill-humor was the amount of good hard money he had frittered away without getting one inch closer to the goal that spurred his every ambition. First there was no small sum he'd given Flaurity for getting old Tarnell out of the way—and he was far from certain it was Flaurity who'd done it; then there was the extra cash it continually cost him to keep the fool on the Tarnell payroll so that he might keep informed of what went on there. There was the money, too, that Cranston had cost him. Good hard cash thrown down the spout. Flame was still putting him off—still stalling. And he had just made an astounding discovery: he was actually becoming *interested* in the girl!

It was phenomenal in a man of his cold temperament. He had never felt the desire that actuated Krell, for instance. Krell's many and varied affairs had only curled his lips in scorn. He'd told Krell more than once to quit mixing women and business. And here he was in Krell's own stable.

It was incredible!

Particularly when he thought of how she'd turned him down three times hand-running! *That,* of course, was Andros' doings! She was nuts about the fellow—and him too dumb to savvy!

He poured another drink from the bottle. Damn bad habit, whisky.

He drank, and his scowl grew blacker as he thought of Andros. Things had been going sweet till that damned drifting gunslick had stumbled in. Why had he come here? Why did he stay? What was there in it for him? Flame Tarnell hadn't hardly more than enough to keep her taxes paid. She couldn't be paying the man in money. . . .

He jerked straight up of a sudden, jolted by a nasty thought. So *that* was the way of it, was it? His cheeks took fire from the fury in him. The tumbler cracked in his hand and with a curse he hurled it from him. Sell him out, would she? By God, he'd show her! He'd get her ranch and he'd get her, too!

It was commentary on Barstow's character that he no longer thought of marrying Flame. He would get what he wanted and afterwards it might be amusing to see what Krell would do with her. Krell had a way with women.

Barstow smiled a little, wickedly. All dogs had their day. Andros' luck should cost him high. God, how he hated that drifting gun-packer! It was the man's cool, easy imperturbability that first had roused his antagonism; but he would think of a way to humble him. If Krell and Flaurity between them weren't sufficient to rid him of the fellow, some other means should be found.

He thought of several ingenious tricks himself, but discarded them as being too hard or too risky of accomplishment. There was a deterring influence in the remembered look of Andros' stare. Not that he was afraid of the man— *Hell, no!* But there was no getting around the fact that Andros' eyes were the coldest he had ever seen. They had a way of getting inside a man's guard—of turning his boldest resolves to water.

Barstow polished off the bottle and set it down with care. There was a nervous flutter got loose in his chest; he was suddenly taut-strung and short of breath. There was a shake to his hands and he braced them, scowling. And still he listened, hunched like a mouse on the couch, eyes darting.

He saw nothing, heard nothing. The storm lashed down with an increased loudness, and the cold of this room crept into his veins. There were eyes upon him—hard eyes probing. He wrenched his chin around and stared.

Bronc Culebra grinned from the doorway.

Temper blazed from Barstow's eyes. "*Knock* when you want in, damn you!"

"Feelin' proddy, ain't you? Mebbe you ain't sleepin' well—"

"Never mind! What do you want here?"

Dark, lean-carved, Bronc Culebra stepped inside with a panther grace and booted the door shut after him. He got his back against a wall without taking his glance off Barstow. Hooking thumbs in his cartridge belt he regarded his boss with the confidence of one who knew his position well.

"I been doin' a mite of thinkin', Reb. This thing won't last. Gov'ment'll step in sure; if the Pool gets licked we'll get licked too. You been diggin' in on Rockin' T, an' this guy, Andros, won't be likin' it. You got too many irons in the fire."

He shifted his shoulders to a greater comfort. "Been thinkin' about death, mostly, an' how one thing's led into another; an' how Tarnell got killed, an' Cranston, Latham an' Bishop Torril. This range is sure a heap onhealthy."

Barstow's shoulders expressed impatience. "How much longer you figurin' to rant?"

"Not much. I'm buildin' up something' for you, Reb; I'm wantin' you to get the picture." Culebra's eyes showed a fleeting irony. " 'Mong other things I been thinkin' how you got Flaurity switched to the Rockin' T—an' how Tarnell cashed his chips quick after. I'm thinkin' a lot about this Krell that you got made a sheriff around here; an' how you've sudden got sweet on Flame— But mostly, Reb, I been thinkin' it's time I got a raise."

Ruddy color crossed Barstow's face. He surged to his feet.

Culebra smiled coldly. "Of course," he said, "I'm appreciatin' how you hev elevated me to Torril's place. But eighty bucks is chicken feed to a guy that's got a mind like mine. Kinda strikes me, Reb, I'd be a pretty good ranny for you to keep around."

"You tryin' to blackmail me?"

"I don't see no call fer ugly words," Culebra said.

Barstow watched him a minute, darkly. "Suppose I don't— Why, you damn' whelp! I'm payin' you more'n you're worth right now!"

"That's a matter of opinion." Culebra set one hand on the handle of his sixshooter. "I could trade notions easy with the Rockin' T—with this guy, Andros. With the Gov'ment, mebbe —I expect they'd be some interested in you. I ain't no fool, Barstow! There's somethin' on that Tarnell spread you're wantin' mighty bad, I'm allowin'. What one guy can find, another can, too. Better think my proposition over."

Barstow's breath was a harsh-pulled sound. "How much?"

"How much you got?— Well, hell," Culebra's grin was a cool, bland thing, "I ain't no plain damn robber, Reb. I expect five grand would do . . . fer now."

Barstow's stare glittered ominously. "For now, eh? An' tomorrow, I guess—"

"I wouldn't be worryin' about tomorrow, Reb. You mightn't be round tomorrow."

"You mightn't yourself. I'm not payin', friend." Barstow grinned across his folded arms.

Culebra also smiled a little.

Rain made the only sound in the room.

Restlessness tugged Barstow's lips. Culebra's shifted posture laid its restraint on Barstow. Culebra said, "You'll look pretty good in striped canvas."

A sigh welled out of Barstow. "I was only funnin', Bronc. I'll pay you, of course." He wheeled off toward a desk in the corner. "I've got the money right here now—"

124

He'd got his left hip out of Culebra's sight. He was reaching for it lightning-fast when a whisper of breath from Culebra stopped him, turned him, stayed his hand. His glance jarred after the other man's. All the color fell out of his face.

Andros lounged in the doorway watching them.

18

"I SHOOT TO KILL!"

WITH AN impatient curse Vargas wheeled from the rain-lashed blackness of the window and crossed to stand bitter-faced above the table where paper fragments made a lettersize square, white against the dusty wood. He grimly gathered the scraps and stowed them in a pocket of his shirt and stood a while longer, scowling. He worried a snatch from some doleful tune. A tough man, Vargas, and one quick to recognize that fibre in his fellows.

A vaquero-garbed man stamped in, dripping water. "We'ave buried—"

Vargas said, "Send in that new ranny—that fellow, Bandera."

The man touched his forelock and left without words. The sound of his bootsteps squelched away.

Vargas lay down on the pine-slat bunk and thought of the message on the torn-up letter. The door groaned protest and brought his glance up to the man who stepped uncertainly in. Vargas said: "I gave Sandoval orders to kill Cass Bocart. Why hasn't he done it?"

Bandera twirled his hat uneasily. He shrugged and presently told of Sandoval's trap and how that devilman, Andros, had shouted warning as Bocart stepped out. He recounted their later attack on the office, and vividly described the black-clad gringo crouched above his flaming guns. He told it with the ring of truth. He was the man who'd trailed blood down the hall.

Wryness disturbed the set of Vargas' mouth. "Send me Duarte Salas," he said, and the ends of his tawny mustache cast moving shadows across his teeth.

Vargas got up when the man went out. He roved to a pause

125

by the window, throwing his bleak gaze across the yard and fingering the paper he'd stuffed in his pocket. He was that way when Duarte Salas came in with a man behind him who shut the door.

"Who's this?" Vargas asked.

At a sign from Salas the man pulled a damp scrap of paper from inside his poncho. Vargas took it and, without dropping his glance, said: "Where'd this come from?"

The peon shrugged. Salas answered. "It was stuffed in a gun tied on Klauson's horse."

"Klauson? You mean the cook?"

Both men nodded.

"Where's Klauson now?"

Salas put a black cigarette between his cracked lips and smiled.

Lamplight put a gleam of copper about the rims of Red Hat's eyes. His left hand gestured. Salas' companion went out. Vargas' glance met Salas' searchingly. Salas shrugged.

He was a rawboned man with a scraggle of beard on his seamed brown face, and deep squint wrinkles about his black eyes. His clothes were brush-clawed and his bare arms scratched. There was something about him though that spelled efficiency. It was the wicked care he took of his pistol.

"There's rotgut in that cupboard," Vargas said, and watched Salas fetch it. He poured himself a good stiff tumbler. He had known, Vargas thought, better days; he was no cheap greaser to guzzle from a bottle. He drank it neat and when he set the glass down empty his schooled face displayed no reaction. Salas asked, "Have you read it yet?" and his watchful eyes were brightly amused when Red Hat shook his head.

"I don't have to," Vargas said. "There ain't but one man in this country with guts enough to down a sheepman and advertise it. I don't need to read no messages from him."

He put his big hands grim into his pockets and all their knuckles showed against the fabric. "I'm goin' to get that ranny," he promised softly. "But if things were different . . ."

Understanding was a look in Salas' eyes. A remote smile touched his lips and he nodded.

Vargas studied him somberly. Grave Creek's showmanship had ever tended to obscure Salas' virtues. Grave Creek had been the swaggering kind, flamboyant in taste, spectacular in

126

action; Salas' work was done with a quiet efficiency evoking no comment—unnoticed. How much of Grave Creek's success, wondered Vargas, had depended on this man's unseen co-operation?

Far back as Vargas could recall, he'd always thought Grave Creek the man indispensable. But now, with Grave Creek gone, he recalled the many chores given Salas, tough and homely tasks so well concluded Salas' quiet worth had passed unnoticed.

"The men," Salas said, "is getting tired potting rabbits," and looked at Vargas carefully. Through the blue haze of expelled smoke the hush held its own understanding. The steel in Salas' holster shone. It matched the glint in Vargas' stare.

"Round up the boys," he nodded. "We're goin' up after them sheep."

Andros lounged with an easy confidence, empty hands loose-hanging at his sides. His soft voice contrasted mightily to the harsh, wet set of his cheeks. He said, "Mebbe I'm interruptin' something. You were going to shoot that fellow weren't you, Barstow?"

Barstow scowled with a palsied fury. But he jerked his hands away from his belt. He dared not risk a look at Culebra. It seemed that only in the locking of his gaze with Andros' could there be any safety in this for him. Andros had heard some part of their talk; it was plain in his stare that he understood it—the black rage in him was apparent, too. It was there in the tautened lines of his figure, in the far-apart way he's got his feet planted, in the curdling of smoke that was in his gray stare.

Someone's breathing in this quiet room made a raucous sound that sent the pounding of Barstow's pulse to tumult when he recognized it for his own.

Andros said, "I understand there's a fellow on your payroll called Dakota."

Barstow gave a start and stiffened. Shifted thought flashed through his stare and a heightened caution reshaped his cheekbones. "You been misinformed," he grunted, and still dared not look toward Culebra. Desperately he prayed the man would keep still. He spoke again, less certain, more worried. "May be one in the country some place; but there ain't none hangin' his hat round here."

He could almost feel Culebra's grin. But the man did not speak and Andros' stare stayed hard on Barstow.

A cold repression got into his voice. "I think you're lyin', Barstow. The man I'm talkin' of has a bad way with women— most particular with other folks' women. Knowin' your interest in Miz' Tarnell . . ." He let the rest trail off, but Barstow read what was in his mind. He was wheeling to pick up the bottle when Andros said: "It may interest you to know that Flaurity's no longer on the Tarnell payroll."

A sudden chill stopped Barstow stiffly. He stood, locked still, with cheeks gone wooden when he saw that Andros was watching him. "He's not on yours any longer, either," Andros said.

"He never was on mine!" Barstow shouted.

But his voice had a stifled sound even in his own ears; and the remote smile gleaming in Andros' stare did nothing to comfort him. "If he said he was, he lied!" Barstow gritted.

"This country's sure plumb full of liars."

"You don't have to stay here," Barstow blustered. "There's other places—"

Andros nodded. "You'd be well advised to start lookin' 'em over. You got a phone here, ain't you?"

Barstow stared. He nodded, silent; then grudgingly added, "Over there by the desk."

"I'm usin' it," Andros said; and crossed to the phone box ominously. He ground the crank, got the operator and gave a San Carlos number. Putting the receiver back on its hook he stared at Barstow grimly.

A silent cold enveloped the room. Culebra stayed against the wall with cheeks expressionless, pale eyes glinting. Andros sat with seeming carelessness upon a corner of the desk.

Barstow stirred uneasily and moved his hands in a nervous motion against the fabric of his coat. The phone shrilled then with startling loudness. "Yes," Andros said, receiver to ear. "Give me Cass Bocart—*Bocart!* Yeah. . . . Well, get him there right away."

Barstow found the wait oppressive. His mouth got sullen and there came a strained look about the edges of his stare.

Andros said abruptly: "That you, Major? . . . Andros talkin'. Yeah. . . . I'm at Barstow's Half-Circle Arrow— Not any more, it don't; Red Hat's wise." He seemed to be listening for several seconds while the gibbering receiver etched rasps of sound across the silence. "Yeah; I'd clean forgot about it. Red Hat

128

. . ." Then Andros said distinctly: "No matter, don't worry about that. I'm all through here—this country's goin' to bust wide open. Yeah. You heard me right. I'm resignin'—*quitting!* Right now!"

He banged the receiver on the hook and wheeled a bright, hard look at Barstow. His voice drove at Barstow wickedly: "You tell your Dakota he better clear out—an' I got a word for *you!* Keep plumb away from the Rockin' T!"

Barstow glared.

"I'm wise to that Long Rope play with Grave Creek. I'm wise to plenty an' I'm onto your game! You keep clear away from Flame Tarnell!"

Rage tore wild words out of Barstow. "You ain't tellin' *me* what I can do! I'll go where I damn well please, an'—an'—"

It stuck in his throat.

The cold, brash gleam of Andros' stare struck terror through and through him. He cringed, and then, in a last access of rage and hate, he snarled: "I'll get her, goddam you, *an' I'll get her ranch!*"

"I've warned you." A sudden smile curled Andros' lips. "And I shoot to kill. Remember it."

19

"THE PLACE'LL RUN PLUMB RED!"

THE ROOM was dark with the shapes of men when Andros entered. He closed the door and put his back against it, eyeing the gathered brush-poppers with a hard, appraising glance. These were the men—these and their outfits—that must form the nucleus of his wild bunch; these must bear the brunt of the Pool's black anger when it was learned what Andros was up to. Others would direct them—hellbenders he had known along the Trail, pistol slammers. But here in this room were the men who would have to do the work.

He saw Dane Quirt, and Shiltmeyer of the Spur, and Hernbarger, and Trane, the boss of Tadpole. And then he saw a face that sent hope surging through him, the face of a tall, lank man, sun-scorched like an Indian's. This face was back in the shadows, but Andros saw its flash of teeth and felt the years roll off his shoulders. Sam Hackberry, one of the four he'd sent for, a tough and reticent rider who'd seen more misery in his time than all this Four Peaks country together.

Andros murmured, "Howdy, Sam," and saw the grin on Hackberry's face grow broader; but he remained back there in the shadows.

Andros' glance swung to front again, to the wondering faces of these Four Peaks cowmen. "I guess we all know what we're up against," he said. "If the sheep come through again we're licked—an' they're comin'. Vargas has gone after 'em."

"How do you know that?" Quirt said in an utter quiet.

"Vargas," Andros told them, "has been camped south of Boulder Mountain. I been over there. He's not there now. He's headin' for White Mountains—may be on his way back now. The trail I cut was six days' old."

"You're sure 'twas Vargas?—Red Hat?"

"It was Red Hat. He's been lookin' out the lay of things. He's with the Pool, of course, an' the Pool sets considerable store by takin' over this country. The Pool don't want no National Forests, an' they got no use for two-bit cow-nurses. It's Vargas' job to run us out."

There was a sullen rumble of thickened voices. Through this cut a high-pitched groan. In a nasal twang somebody said, "Boys, this is terrible bad."

"Bad!" Andros said with anger. "If the whole damn push of you don't get back of me to do something about it this range is finished!"

"Don't see's there's anything we kin do about it," Quirt said dubiously, and Shiltmeyer shook his grizzled head. "There ain't, Dane. This country's seen the last of cattle. We've fit Injuns, rustlers, drought an' hoemen. We can call all the critters we've got by name."

Old Hernbarger muttered, "In der Vatterlandt dey vould nod stand for dis. Vere iss your pragged-of vreedoms, hein? Py Gott, we ain'dt got noddings pot plood und pullets!"

Andros' gaze whipped hard to Trane. Trane shrugged his saddle-bowed shoulders. "We ain't got the dinero to see this through even if there was sense in it. It takes hard cash to wad a gun." He shook his head without anger. "Was we to try toughin' it out against these sheepmen, it would be like askin' what they give Jack Broth las' year. Jack was a heller, but

130

short on savvy. Reckon there'll be a mort of us pullin' out next two-three days. . . . I'd sure like t' see it diff'rent, but . . ." He shrugged; held out his hand. "I'm wishin' you luck, stranger."

"Yellow, eh?"

Obe Trane scowled and the tips of his ears changed color. He looked down at the hand he'd held out, and gingerly rubbed it across the frazzled corduroy of his pants. "Them's fightin' words, friend. I've seen the day—"

Cold frost rode Andros words: "When the rest of the stove-up has-beens has pulled their freight an' said good night, the rest of us'll get down to business."

No one moved nor, apparently, did anyone resent that tone; nor the fleering curl of Andros' lips. "Okey," he drawled. "Tuck in your tails an' get to your slinkin'—I'll manage to make out some way. But I wish to Christ there was a couple of *men* in this locality! I ain't askin' for any real double-actin' engines —just a couple one-armed swampers is all I need to get by on."

Quirt flushed. "Y'u got no call to—"

"A-ah!" sneered Andros, "get to hell on outa here— *all of you!* I got a couple rustlin' friends I reckon'll help me out in this!"

"We tried—" Shiltmeyer started to bleat; but Andros cut him off with a snort.

"You wouldn't know a try if it kicked you in the pants!"

Sam Hackberry spoke from the shadows. "What you got in mind, friend?"

"Nothin' you'd be interested in. No use my wastin' any more breath. It's more'n a fellow should expect to get a show of spunk from a bunch of sod-turnin' squatters—"

"I don't take that kind of yap off *no* man!" Trane blazed hotly.

"Don't make me laugh! Go on—clear out, you bunch of frayed-out scarecrows! I'd rather have your room. I'll get me some Digger Injuns!"

"Well, spill your guts," Quirt muttered. "We'll listen a bit—"

"I don't need no audience—what I want is *fightin'* men! Som—"

Trane snarled: "Say what you got us here for!"

"My plan's to scatter," Andros said, still scowling. "Scatter an' peck at these Pool outfits till they—"

"Raidin'!" jeered Quirt, disgustedly. "Might's well pop at 'em

131

with a fly-swatter! I thought you had some kind of *plan!* Why, they'd larrup us off this range so quick we'd never know what struck us! C'mon, boys; let's git home."

Straight and solid Andros blocked the door. "Go on," he said. "I couldn't use you no how. This is *men's* work—an' I guess I savvy where to get 'em—"

"You'll get no men round here," Quirt snarled, "that's fool enough to back you in no such damn foolishness as—"

"I'll get Rockinstraw, Ed Tailman, New River Ned, Sam Hackberry, an' Kid Badger!"

The hush that gripped these ranchers showed the power of those five names. They were the five most wanted gun-fighters on any sheriff's list. Outlaws all—notorious from the Panhandle to Nevada. Rewards on them, if paid would have run to fabulous figures. They were the worst of the Border Riders —men close associated with the bloody histories of the Southwest's unhealthiest sections. Names to be feared and whispered.

"God A'mighty!" Obe Trane cried. "You'd bring them *here?*—them *hellions?*"

"I've sent for them."

"Caesar's ghost!" breathed Quirt, his voice pitched like a prayer. "Might's well turn red Injuns loose an' be done with it! You gone stark ravin' mad?"

"Mad enough to give that Pool a dose of its own damn medicine! I'm goin' to give 'em what they gave Teal's Flowerpot. There's just one way to beat this bunch—it's a way I'm goin' to take!"

Lamplight piled the shadows darkly across his tautened cheeks. He stood with thumbs hooked in gun belts, regarding them with bitter eyes. "It's not a thing I would or *could* do if I was hooked up with the National Forest movement—or any other kind of accepted law. But I'm not; an' this is cattle country! By the grace of God I'm goin' to see it stay that way!"

"Hell's fire!" Quirt snapped, "they'll never come. An' if they did—"

"They won't! What could he offer 'em?" another growled.

"I'm offerin' them nothing," Andros answered. "Sheep put those men where they are. Sheep will bring 'em back—"

Shiltmeyer shouted. "You're crazy as a loon!" And Quirt buttoned his coat and looked at Trane significantly. Trane nodded, pulling on his gloves, and turned bent shoulders doorward.

Andros cursed them bitterly. "You fools! Sam Hackberry's here right now!" He flung his glance across their heads to a flash of teeth in the shadows. "For God's sake, Sam, help me talk sense into 'em!"

Sam Hackberry's voice came dry as dust.

"Clem's right, the boys will come," he said. "Needn't to worry about that part. We been waitin' too all-fired long t' git a lick at them sheepmen."

Stillness stiff as a drumhead followed.

A man's spurs harshly rasped the floor. Old Hernbarger's. He stopped beside Andros solidly. "Py Gott," he wheezed, "you god some pullets for mine gon?"

"I'll buy you a cartload," grinned Andros tightly; and kept his look hard upon the crowd. Here and there a man's glance sheepishly slid away.

Quirt's uneasy look said he did not like it. Trane said with the solemn care of a man deep-thinking: "Let's have the rest of it."

"Get your kids an' womenfolks some place safe. From here out this is goin' to be wolf eat wolf. Cut loose of everything; there'll be no holds barred. My way ain't goin' to be easy, but it's the only thing there's left to do. Them that rides with me ain't goin' to have no time to look out for belongings.

"You'll have to let your spreads take care of themselves. Some may get burnt; but as things stand right now the sheepmen'll get 'em anyway. Cut an' run, is my plan—hard an' fast. We've got to band into bunches an' I'll pick the leaders. I'm pickin' Sam Hackberry here, an' New River Ned, Art Rockinstraw, Tailman an' Kid Badger. Them as don't like it can pull out now an' take their chances. Anyone quittin' later will get plugged sudden."

Shiltmeyer swore aghast. "Them hellions will pull this country plumb apart! Nothin'll stop 'em—*nothin'!* This country'll go clean up in smoke—"

"But it'll still be ours. The sheep will go up with it."

Shiltmeyer stared. "Good Christ, the place'll run plumb red!"

Andros said, "I hope so."

20

COIN OF THE REALM

EXPERIENCED in the ways of big outfits with smaller competitors, it was not at all hard for Andros to understand the dread in which these cowmen held the Pool. No luke warm measures had built it. Only by the speedy piling of disaster on top of disaster could the Pool be licked.

Andros' plans were brief and simple. The money Bocart had given him was swiftly converted into pistol and rifle fodder. Had Vargas thought to search his hat that roll would have gone the way of his wallet. But Vargas hadn't—or rather, he hadn't had time to once the thought struck him. Sam Hackberry proved invaluable with shrewd suggestions. Andros avoided Flame Tarnell whenever he could. He had not forgotten her parting words that night he rode to Barstow's.

His meeting with the small-spread cowmen took place on the night of August's last Tuesday. By Wednesday night all his owlhoot riders had come in but Tailman, and they had word of him. Kid Badger had brought six friends along, tough and reckless Texans who considered this business a lark.

With twenty men Andros set to work. Saturday night the first blow was struck; northwest of Mocking Bird Pass, in the heart of the timber country.

Lamplight, spilling from the windows of the super's office and from the low rough shanties flanking it, filtered through the shaggy pines, driving golden rays through the crowding dark flung down by a moonless night. Dark-garbed riders statuesquely sat their ponies in the screening brush and studied the clearing without comment.

Sixteen sawmills whined and snorted. This was headquarters camp for the great Southwestern lumber syndicate which in whirlwind strides had already denuded twenty miles of ranching country. It was the largest timber interest in the Pool.

Sam Hackberry, watching the screeching sheds, said, "Got a mort o' ridin' starin' us in the face tonight, boys. Take them sawmills first. Then the shacks. I'll handle the Super's office. Watch out fer the women an' brats. Cold Water Crick an' Dry Cimarron next." He sent a last raking glance across the open, shifted his cud and spat. "Let's get at it."

The eastern sky was brushed with pink, the land's dark contour shoving against it like the hackles of an angry dog. A long file of horsemen drifted down the rimrock toward where a group of cabins vaguely showed through the thinning murk. The ponies moved on muffled feet and only the rhythmic creak of chaps and saddle leather disturbed the morning's stillness.

A faint down-draft from the tumbled hills carried the smell of lifted dust, and sheep—thousands of them—covered the valley like a soiled gray blanket, a fuzzy huddle against the earth. There was a dozing horse before the largest cabin; if it heard or sensed the approaching riders it gave no sign.

In a great thin circle the dark horsemen wheeled, quick spacing their broncs, taking what cover offered as Hackberry rode up to the cabin where the horse stood. Brightening day gleamed dully on the barrels of lifted carbines.

Hackberry's .45-.90 drove a slug through the cabin door.

Men spewed forth like angry wasps to blink and halt confused midstride when they saw the ring of watching riders. "Figurin' to move them sheep?" asked Hackberry casually, and the sheepmen's eyes went slitted.

"You're goddam right we are!"

"That's fine. We're here to help y'u," Hackberry said. "Jest turn them blatters round an' head 'em back through the Pass." He jerked his rifle nozzle north.

The sheep boss laughed. He was pretty tough. "You go to—"

Flame licked out of Hackberry's rifle. The sheepman licked his lips. "There's a law in this country, hombre—"

"Y'u bet!" said Hackberry. "Gun law—it's lookin' y'u spang in the eye!"

There was a shifting in the sheepmen's ranks. But they knew the courts were back of them. The sheep boss snarled while his hombres eased hands beltward. "The courts—"

"Will be a leetle mite late t' do "y'u fellas much goods," drawled Hackberry. "Ed, get this outfit's burros packed. Jack, y'u an' two-three the other boys get them blatters movin'. 'F

135

they don't move fast enough mebbe y'u better burn some powder."

The sheep boss scowled. He was over-gunned at the moment; and he knew well what his owners would say if he let these cowpunchers shoot his sheep. He glared at Hackberry poisonously. "We'll move 'em. I was on'y funnin' any—"

"Me, too," drawled Hackberry drily. "I'll be funnin' a dang sight harder if I catch y'u comin' back."

Horse Mountain was a blaze of heat and sun's glare bright upon its crags when three men rounded a bend in the trail and pulled up under a towering pine that stood forty feet from a ranch house. The leader of this trio dismounted and hammered a white piece of paper to the tree's bole with his pistol butt. While he backed, inspecting it, his companions sniggered.

A swart and stocky man came off the veranda at a lope, and an angular man came after him, throwing talk back over his shoulder. The strange riders completely ignored them. Shoving forward, the chunky man stared narrowly at his tree's new sign. With a lurid oath he jerked about and shouted: "Keal! Stafferd!" He flung a brash look at the strangers. "What's the big idea?"

"Read, can'tcha?"

"No slat-eyed Mormon bastard is goin' to move—"

"Ain't this the Keyhole horse spread?"

"No!" the chunky sheepman snarled. "Not no more, it ain't! We done taken it over. This outfit's a holdin' of the Kelsadine Sheep Cor—"

"A part of Vargas' outfit, eh?"

"What about it?" The chunky man paused, took another look at the short man facing him. "Say, ain't you the squirt they call Art Rockin—"

"I reckon y'u know me, Kelsey. Get yo' traps together."

"You—" The sheepman made as though to step backward. He stopped with a gun barrel digging his belly. Few men lived who could whip a gun from leather quicker than Art Rockinstraw. Fear beaded Kelsey's brow with sweat; he threw a tortured look at the lanky man who had come with him off the veranda. But the lanky man was earnestly directing his attention at the cloudless sky; he was not interested in things mundane.

136

Kelsey's bloated face was purple. You could almost smell the rage in him. He said gratingly, "You can't get away with this, Rockinstraw!"

Perhaps it was the hurried pound of booted feet that made him brash and belligerent in the face of Rockinstraw's pistol. He slammed his words like the flat of an ax. "By Gawd, you'll never cut it!"

Two men came round a corner of the barn. There were pistols in their lifted fists. They were a pair of Kelsey's sheep hands and they sized things up at a glance.

Kelsey clawed for leather. Four guns roared out at once and Kelsey, with his gun half drawn, lurched round and fell like a pole-axed steer. One of Rockinstraw's boys dropped forward across his saddle cursing, and was dragged off by his pitching bronc. Rockinstraw struck the hammer of his trig- gerless gun again. The ball went through the head of the nearest sheepman; he crumpled up by the toolshed. His com- panion whirled with a choking scream and tried to get behind the barn again, but Rockinstraw knocked him down in his tracks.

There was something fierce and blazing in the look Rock- instraw gave the lanky man who still stood with his hands straight up. Gun sound rolled around the yard, smashed like ball bats against the buildings. Rockinstraw said: "Git goin', fella—git goin' quick."

The lank man's lips writhed whitely. His face was like bleached paper. "But—I can't!" he groaned. "The sheep—"

"Y'u want a bullet through yore guts?" Rockinstraw did not wait for an answer. He struck the hammer of his gun. "Let's get at them goddam woolies now!" he said to the man still with him.

Andros thought it would take Vargas' men another two days to get the main flocks down from the mountains onto the Cottonwood. Assured of this he had sent his raiders far afield, scattering their activities from the Prescott ranges to the White Ledges below Soldier Creek—and north as far as Long Valley.

Always the sheepmen's comings and goings had been timed to the rains and the coming of grass. Feed brought up by the winter rains had been gouged to the roots by sheep working northward into the White Mountains. Now with fall just

137

around the corner, Vargas' men would ease these sheep back, feeding off what grass these recent storms had pulled from the stubborn earth.

Andros was right; but he miscalculated Red Hat's speed.

This morning, backed by a crew of nervous Four Peaks cowmen, he had ridden to the flanking hogback above the Cottonwood, and there had left them to hold it just in case the sheep came early. "Dig in here an' if the sheep come, fight—but hold this ridge till I can get some men in to help you. Whatever you do don't let them sheep pass." He had gone off then with New River Ned; and hardly had he gone from sight when the sheep hit Asher's Basin.

The move showed Vargas' foresight. He had expected that hogback to figure in Andros' plans and had cunningly avoided it. He had crossed Salt River away up yonder and had run his sheep through Brown's place, feeding it down to the roots. And now their dirty white ribbon was snaking through the pass from Asher's Basin—a stinking, blatting stream of gray—a flood that spilled across green-carpeted uplands with the appetite of starving locusts.

Band after band surged bleating from the pass. The sound of their cropping teeth and cutting hooves made little more noise than the wings of buzzards sailing round above them, waiting for the guns to bark.

Andros' cowmen left the hogback when the first sheep smell came down the wind. They cut for the timber with quirt and spur, dragging out with stunned minds reeling before the crashing fragments of their useless hopes.

But deep in the midst of the sheepmen's laughter, a big and high-powered rifle spoke. The bullets came from such distance only a faint popping sound reached the sheepmen's ears. But the bullets came with plenty of force. One swarthy sheepman sprang to his feet with a frightened curse as lead ripped the skillet out of his hands. The bunched sheep made a splendid target, a target the rifleman was quick to spot. All across the bedground sheep dropped. The rest scuttled frantically downslope as the cursing herders sprang to saddle. The flocks ran wild and no one stopped them; that man with the rifle was too fine a shot. The herders flew to protect their own hides.

The X.O.G., a cattle syndicate that months earlier had

taken over Ed Tailman's range, was holding a large gather of beef in the vicinity of Spaulding Spring, fattening up for the approaching fall market. It was eleven P.M. and only the smoldering embers of the cook's dying fire illumined the starless night. Around the wagon a score of men made dark shapes in their blankets, their rising snores giving testimony of a day hard spent at work.

A crash of gunfire roused the night. Belching guns shot streaks in the sky. One instant later every steer was up, afoot with snorts and frightened bawlings. Dust swirled about them, and muzzleflame sheared at the bedground from thirteen points southeast of camp.

The beef herd lifted tails and ran. Shrill screams, hot lead and high-pitched whoopings hustled them into a lumbering gallop.

Faster and faster the wild hooves pounded. The terrified steers with lowered heads went humping for Leonard Canyon in a crazy charge that could not be turned nor ever stopped.

21

"I'M COMIN' FOR YORE HIDE!"

ALL ACROSS three mighty counties men scarce dared to draw their breath for fear of stopping ambush lead. Word from a dozen places reached the Barstow ranch of havoc wrought by raiding horsemen. The Four Peaks country flew with rumor that Black Clem Andros was fighting the Pool.

Badly shaken, Barstow stayed in his ranch house brooding. From the San Carlos Reservation in the east, to Mormon Flat in the west, clear north to the Tule Butte range, war guns were cracking and the song of lead drowned out all others. The Limestone Hills were splotched with blood. Bloated carcasses were polluting the waters of Twenty-Nine-Mile Lake. Sawmill had seen fighting. There were no buildings left at Schoolhouse Tank. Leonard Canyon was filled with dead cattle. On Wildcat Hill three men dangled stiffly on hempen ropes attached to tall pines. A surveyor's party from the railroad had bucked ambush guns and were left where they'd fallen. Cave Creek Village was a ghost town after a five-minute raid by a dozen masked horsemen. Tortilla Camp was a buzzards' rendezvous, acrid and nauseous with the stench of dead sheep. There was talk of calling in the soldiers—only those who needed them most had no excuse for the calling.

Red Hat Vargas was raising hell. Already two larruping horsemen had come pelting to Barstow with messages from him. He demanded to know why Barstow was holding back. His far-flung flocks were being scattered by the slashing forays of Andros' raiders. The Pool was strong as ever, he said, but he needed more men and he needed them *now*. The first of that Barstow would not believe; he believed the last part too well. He told the messenger his crew had quit him. Quick as he could get others he would hasten with them to Red Hat's aid—that was what he told the first man. To the second messenger Barstow explained, exasperated, that he could not get men at *any* price; that, perforce, he must stay and guard his ranch.

Culebra, after this last man left, strolled grinning from the bunkhouse for a look at Barstow's face. "Next time," he taunted slyly, "it'll be Red Hat comin' himself. You better decide what you're goin' to say to him."

To which Barstow said not a word. He clamped his lips and tramped inside and slammed the door behind him.

But Bronc Culebra was proved a true prophet within the next five hours.

Barstow had himself in hand. He nodded curtly when Vargas strode in; he ignored Culebra's sly smile entirely. He pushed a bottle across his desk and Red Hat knocked it flying. But Barstow got his talk in first. "I was sure relieved to hear you got them brush-poppers licked," he stated. "Looked for awhile like you mightn't cut it."

"Happens I ain't *got* them licked." Vargas' smile was completely unpleasant. "I want to know why you refused to send help when I asked for it—an' why you got ten fellas posted around outside with rifles. A guy ain't short-handed when he can afford that many ornaments."

"Them men are there," Barstow said, "to protect my property. They're men I've just now hired—which I was goin' to bring up to stiffen your hand just as quick's you got another messenger here so's I'd know where the hell to take 'em."

"I always figured you for a belly-crawlin' snake, Reb," Vargas told him. "Nothin' you've said makes me change my mind."

Barstow's ears showed a risen color. His head tipped a little slanchways and threw one look at Culebra who was stiff against the left-hand wall.

"You're the kind," Vargas said, "that figures to let some other fool rake your chestnuts out of the fire for you."

"You can talk," Barstow gritted thickly. "You ain't got money tied up in buildings—"

"I've got *sheep*, by Christ!" Red Hat bellowed. "An' I been seein' a hell's passle of 'em shoved over canyons an'—"

"Exactly!" Barstow grunted. "Think I want to see my cattle—"

"It's too damned bad about your cattle! You're in this or you ain't, by God! If you are, I want your help—*right now!* Am I gettin' it or not?"

Barstow's face showed a strong dislike. "You're gettin' a little brash, friend, ain't you? I'm as much in this Pool as you are—more, I shouldn't wonder. If this was any other time I'd be tellin' you to go plumb to hell. As it is, I'm sidin' the Pool," Barstow said, "like always."

Vargas nodded. "This is a damn good time to prove it. We've got Andros' crowd bottled up in Hell's Hip Pocket. You can back up your good intentions by collectin' them outside rifles an' ridin' up there with me—now."

Culebra's chuckle crossed the silence; and when he saw their wheeled expressions he guffawed, loud and heartily.

"What's so funny?" Vargas said.

"This whole damn' business." Culebra grinned sardonically. "Ain't y'u found out yet Reb's great intentions is things to be *aired*, not acted? Ain't y'u savvied all he's wantin' is Tarnell's Rockin' T?"

Vargas looked at Barstow carefully, a strange glint in his half-closed stare. "All the old man owned is three hundred acres. What would Reb be wantin' with that? Goin' to take to gardenin', is he?"

"He's got a mighty itch for land, Reb has," Culebra told him. "Partic'lar that land. He's spent more nights pokin' round there than a feller could shake a stick at. He's—" Culebra broke off suddenly, shoved free of the wall. One bunched fist burst above his holster. There was danger in his

141

tense, splayed fingers. Danger to match the rage of Barstow.

The cowman's bloated face was livid; but if Culebra couldn't share the wealth, he was determined Barstow should not, either. "This bastard," he said, looking straight at Reb, "has found *oil* on the Rockin' T!"

There was brutal fury in Barstow's snarl. His hand made a white streak slapping hipward. Outward flame leaped, blue and wicked.

Culebra's face went a haggard gray and all the lines of it stretched—contorted. He swayed in the lamplight, trying to trigger. But Barstow's payoff lead had tagged him. His bent form broke at the knees and toppled.

Barstow's gun was covering Vargas. The lust for blood blazed out of his stare. "*You* wantin' some?" he snarled at him thickly.

Vargas said "No," softly, and did not move so much as an eyelid. "Comin' with me, are you?"

Sweat was a shine on Barstow's forehead and madness still glared bright from his eyes. "I'm through with your goddam Pool!" he snarled. His gun motioned Vargas toward the door. "One word o' this an' I come for your hide! Now get out, by God, an' don't come back!"

22

CUPID BUILDS A LOOP

PARTING with Ed Tailman Thursday morning on the assurance that all his raiders were working overtime, Andros rode south from Shake Tree Canyon and moved on down Deer Creek toward the stream's intersection with Maple Draw. Rocking T was in his mind and he strove to plan some decisive blow that should smash the Pool at one fell stroke. But Flame Tarnell was before his thoughts and he only knew that, somehow, it had become terrifically important that they bury the hatchet and be friends again. It made no difference that time and again these last few days he had called himself all kinds of a fool ever to think they could be friends again. He was going to see her anyway; something stronger than himself was shoving him ranchward.

He reached headquarters just after noon. Three punchers lounged by the bunkhouse with .45-.90s across their laps. Coldfoot grinned. The other two held their cheeks wooden and watched him warily. Andros swung down. "Better work a little bit farther out. Spur was burned to the ground last night."

He trailed his reins and walked to the ranch house. At the porch he wheeled abruptly and crossed to the mess shack, passing straight through to the kitchen back of it. No one was round, but he found what he wanted and carried it to the table in the outer room.

He gulped the food in hungry haste and was clearing his throat with a swig of cold coffee when a shadow crossed the mess-shack floor. His quick swing found Grace Latham in the doorway, sun's glare outlined her limber figure. "What you doin' here?" he asked ungraciously.

Her lips framed a twisted smile. She said, "You sure are glad to see me," but no resentment looked out of her eyes. She came toward him leaving the door standing open.

She stood for a long time staring down at him. Her voice was thoughtful—just a little protesting, when she said, "I guess you've seen me about all you aim to . . ."

He looked up then. She met his glance defiantly. "I didn't come here hunting you—Gallup John brought me out last night. Seemed to think it wasn't safe for me in town." She smiled a little, wistfully.

"Where's Gallup now?"

"Off raidin' with your crowd, I guess. Soon's he got me here he went tearing off with three-four others—I think one of them was the man they call Kid Badger." She said with some obscure thought lighting up her eyes, "Folks are beginning to learn that you're around. They're saying in town if you keep this up another week all the two-bit ranchers in the country will get behind you. My gamblers are placing odds of five to one you'll break the Pool."

"Gallup John," Andros said, "thinks a powerful lot of you."

The brightness left her eyes; left an odd expression in them. She rested one hip on the table and her dangling foot made tiny motions in the air. She said rebelliously: "If I'd wanted Gallup John I could have had him long ago. Why don't you use your eyes for a change?"

143

She leaned abruptly forward, pointed breasts swaying two sharp patterns against the fabric of her blouse. "Why can't you like me?" she cried miserably. "Aren't we both lone wolves? Why can't you see in me what it is you're after? God knows I've plenty to give a man—why don't you *want* me?"

He didn't immediately answer. A stillness fell between them. He pulled a long breath into his chest and got up. "It's not what I want or don't want, Grace; it's the way things have got to be. It's facts we've got to reckon with and they've got me pegged for a killer. You don't want that kind of man."

"How do you know what I want?"

"I know what wouldn't be good for you. A man can't go behind the record of six years. The things a man does catch up with him. When the things I've done catch up with me, I'll face 'em by myself."

"I'd be glad to share them, Clem—"

"It won't work, Grace."

"What about Flame Tarnell?"

He stared and felt his cheeks go hot. He said angrily, "I ain't askin' her to marry me!"

Her laugh was harsh. "You know better! She wouldn't wipe her feet on you—do you know what she calls you? *Gun fighter!* She hasn't the sense to know you're takin' God's only way to save her range! Her and her Sunday-school mind! What does *she* know about love? Do you think she could really *love* anyone? Don't be a fool, Clem Andros!"

She looked at him boldly, willfully. "I can give a man what he wants—"

Andros said with taut, pale cheeks, "Love ain't a thing you can shift at will—" and her tinkle of laughter mocked him.

"I've read that in the copybooks, too." She put a hand on his arm; leaned toward him. "Don't you know it's sheer animal magnetism that backs nine out of every ten marriages? What could Flame Tarnell ever bring you? Why, you'd play hell every time you—"

He slapped her hard across the face, his cheeks dead white with anger. "Don't speak her name again!"

Then the rage fell out of him. He looked at her, shocked. She was actually smiling. She swung off the table, leaned forward eagerly. He felt the bulge of her breasts against him, the pull of her arms. "Oh, *Clem*—" It was the whisper of Eve, and Eve's spell was on him.

144

With an oath he caught her arms from around him, forced them down. "Flame's puttin' you up here, ain't she?"

"What of it? She'd do the same for a dog—I owe her nothing for that!" She broke his grip. Her arms went round his neck again, pulling his head down with all her strength, forcing his mouth hard against her own.

He got the flats of his hands against her shoulders and was bracing himself to shove her loose when a shadow blocked the open door. Across Grace's shoulder he saw Flame's white face. One moment he saw it and then she was gone.

The sound of an oncoming horse finally roused Andros. Grace Latham was against the table and he stood, not seeing her, with shoulders bowed. The horse sound stopped in the yard outside. A rider's boots struck dirt and skidded. The door burst open. A wild-eyed rider stood peering in. He cried affrightedly: "Sam Hackberry's dead!"

Andros stared at him numbly.

The man said, "God sakes! Can't you *hear* me? Sam Hackberry's dead on Methodist Mountain—near cut in two! An' there's six of his boys layin' riddled there with 'im!"

23

BARSTOW

VARGAS tossed his reins across the peeled pole fronting Latham's saloon and stepped inside with his hat cuffed low. If he enjoyed the way all talk fell off at his appearance he did not show it. A barman hurried forward to serve him. Vargas asked for Barstow and the barman's thumb indicated a back room. Vargas crossed to the door and went in, kicking the door shut after him. Barstow was there and Krell, the sheriff, leaned against a wall at the room's far side. A single lamp shed sickly light. Vargas said, "You wanted to see me?" and Barstow nodded. He shoved a note across the table silently, his glittering eyes on Vargas' face.

Red Hat picked up the note and read it. "I've found out what you been wanting with the Rocking T. Better leave that oil alone." A single name was signed to the scrawl—*Andros.*

Vargas, lifting chin, saw Barstow watching him. The glint of Barstow's eyes had changed. Trouble feel was in this place. Krell was shifting weight with a straining care. Vargas said, "You don't think *I* told him, do you?"

"Somebody did!" Barstow gritted; and the hand on his gun butt showed white knuckles. Krell leaned a little forward.

Vargas said, "I see you've told Krell. Mebbe Krell told Andros."

Krell said wickedly, "Yeah—an' mebbe he *didn't!"*

Red Hat's lips showed a faint kind of smiling, and he put the flats of his hands down gently on the table. The room felt cold and brittly taut as though this stillness were stretched beyond endurance.

Barstow stooped. "I got a way with sidewinders." When he straightened there was a gun in each hand.

Fury was bright in Vargas' eyes. One hand whipped under his coat and came out. Detonation bulged the room. Smoke was a blue fog swirling crazily. It was thick round Barstow's low-crouched shape. It curled from the gun in Krell's lean hand. Not a shot ever left Vargas' pistol. He fell with its hammer still at half-cock.

Less than a minute later Barstow came into the barroom through the swinging doors of the big front entrance. The barman who'd directed Red Hat looked up and his face went grayly blank. His swabbing hand left off all movement. Some of the customers who'd been inquiringly staring toward the back room's door, looked around.

Barstow said with a cold thin smile, "Seen anything of Vargas, Halpin? He sent me word to meet him here. Where is he?"

The barman stood like a blight had struck him. He jerked his head at the back room's door. "He—he went in there, Mister Barstow."

Barstow turned on his heel and went coolly down a room gone quiet, watched by the customers' completest attention. He did it well. He went to the door and tried the knob. "Huh —locked!" he muttered, and pounded its panels with peremptory fist. He waited a moment, then banged again. "You sure?" he said across a shoulder—"sure he went in here?"

The barman nodded. "He—he sure did. I saw 'im, didn't I?" he appealed to the custom.

Barstow, grunting, drew back one shoulder. "No sense

146

bustin' the door down," a voice said quietly. "There's another door round at the back."

Barstow looked at this man coldly. "Mebbe you better go an' try it."

The house man went out.

Barstow looked at his watch. He said to the putty-faced barman: "If Red Hat's in there, tell him I'll be back. I've a chore down the street—won't take but a minute."

Saloon lamps drove yellow bars across the street's blackness. Andros, facing Latham's hitchrack, stepped out of the saddle and looked to his guns. Sheathing them he stood for a moment among the shadows, eying the gaunt shack's dust-grimed windows. Ten-fifteen, Barstow's note had said. It was ten-twelve now. He could recall every word of Barstow's message. "Meet me at Latham's at ten-fifteen. I believe we can end this feuding pronto. If you fail to come, responsibility for all further killings will rest with you. I'm doing this account of Flame."

Andros had come account of Flame, too. He well knew what danger might conceivably attend his open appearance on any town's street. Barstow's note had the smell of a baited trap. But he had to make sure—this thing *might* be straight. Barstow, now that his oil grabbing scheme was exposed, just *might* be tricky enough to swap sides. He might hope to smooth things over and get that oil by marriage.

Andros' shoulders stirred impatiently. He would damn soon know.

He mounted the steps to the saloon veranda. A buzz of excitement came through the batwings. He pushed through them swiftly—got his back to a wall. Latham's custom was congregated about some intensely interesting thing on the bar. Andros could not see what this was; but he noticed one man who was not with the others. A tall wasp-waisted man with his face shaved so close his blue jowls shone. He stood at one end of the polished bar. A smaller man held the other end. Both watched Andros with a sly regard. Then the little man started toward him. He said, "Howdy, pardner. Hev y'u got the makin's?"

Andros saw the Durham tag dangling from the man's shirt pocket. From the corners of his eyes he saw the tiny

147

shifting of the tall man at the bar's end. With left hand he reached for the sack in his own shirt pocket while he rubbed his jaw with his other hand slowly. "Yeah," he said, and knew there was no change in this pattern. He had stood this way many times before and seen other troubles shaping up toward gunsmoke. He had guessed right. Barstow's note was a trap.

He smiled at the little man thinly and tossed the man his tobacco. His wheeling look caught the tall man in the act of moving forward. The tall man stopped under Andros' look —lowered his lifted foot with solemn care. A scowl swept fleetingly across his face. Andros grinned at him toughly.

One cat-quick step took Andros to where the back-bar's mirror showed the batwings back of him; and he laughed when he saw the face framed there—Barstow's face, black scowling.

The little man had rolled his cigarette. He had it between his lips now with his left hand bringing up a match to light it. He puffed and, grinning, tossed the sack back to Andros. Andros let it fall unheeded. That trick had whiskers that would need a lawnmower. He knew the men before him now —they were Shane and Hodders, the sheriff's deputies—the men he had driven off the Rocking T. He appreciated the gleam in the shorter man's eyes.

Hodders, the tall man, abruptly spoke. "We're arrestin' y'u, Andros. Git your hands up."

Andros stood stiffly planted, unmoving, the planes of his high cheeks bleakly angular. He drawled at Barstow's mirrored reflection. "You won't ever learn, Reb, will you?"

Barstow sneered. "Your goose is cooked."

Andros sighed when he saw the little man's shoulders settling. At the bar's end steel rasped leather. All bets were off; to stall any further would be sheer suicide. Andros drove his right hand legward.

The crash of guns rushed against these walls. Blue fog choked the room and bit men's nostrils. Powder smoke swirled about Andros' bent figure and frantically whipped through a half-raised window. And when it cleared little Shane lay dead; and against the bar the tall man, Hodders, sagged, sobbing curses, both elbows shattered.

Andros turned with a look cold as death. He said dustily, "You can't catch a wolf with skunk traps, Barstow!"

148

His eyes smashed the burly ranchman backwards. "You started this. Now suppose you finish it."

Barstow stared like a man demented.

"You been itchin' to see me planted ever since I hit this country," Andros said. "Quit starin', tinhorn, an' drag that gun!"

Venom flattened Barstow's roan cheeks. But he shook his head. "Not yet, friend. Not just yet."

"Why not? What you waitin' for? Have you always got to see a man's back before you dare put finger to trigger?"

Cold sweat stood on Barstow's forehead. "I can wait for mine," he gritted doggedly.

"Wait till I turn my back, you mean?" Contempt was plain in Andros' look. "I don't think even a polecat would eat from the same plate you use!"

24

"COME A-SMOKIN'!"

FACING his men in the ramshackle cabin at Tournament Flat Andros said: "What we've done we've done pretty well—but it ain't enough. We've got to work faster an' hit a damned sight harder if we aim to smash this Pool."

"Brass tacks," Kid Badger suggested.

"In plain words," Andros said, "the Pool's commencin' to get its breath. They've got more gun fighters an' their riders outnumber us ten to one. We've got by thus far because they've not been organized. We've had the jump on 'em. Fast as they'd lam reinforcements off to some isolated spot, one of our gangs would come down on the place those men were taken from.

"But that's all over; they're set now and our system's pegged. Way they trapped Sam Hackberry shows it. We got one chance left to bust 'em. An' one chance only."

"Let's hear it," said Rockinstraw, clearing his throat.

"We've got to hit at their strongest point. We've got to smash Reb Barstow flat!"

New River Ned whistled softly. "Barstow's got more'n thirty

riders—all tough hands from who laid the chunk. They'll be watchin' for a play like that!"

There were other grumblings. Rockinstraw said, "The whole country will."

"That's why we've got to do it." Andros minced no words. "It's the surest way to crack this Pool. If we can carry it off there won't be enough nerve left in that bunch to pin up a baby's diapers with! You fellows," he looked them over, "used to have pretty hard reps—but nothin' like this Pool will pin on you if they come through on top. If we quit now, or lose, they'll have posses huntin' us from hell to breakfast. What's more they'll have the whole Southwest laughin' at us for a bunch of fool kids that thought we was tough."

That brought them up as nothing else could have. They *were* tough; but not so tough they could stand folks' laughter. Andros said: "Barstow's on the skids right now."

"That don't make me feel no better," New River Ned said scowling, "about bein' made food for the posies tomorrow. Crackpot stunts I'm ready to try; but a stunt like that—Hell! we could never cut it."

"Barstow's shaky," said Andros harshly. "He's scared of his shadow. Three-four of his best men's left him—pulled out complete for other parts. There's talk around his bunkhouse of more of 'em pullin' out. There's others wants to hook up with Vargas' fightin' Chihuahuans—an' Barstow knows it. He can't trust a one of 'em."

Ed Tailman said slowly, "How d'you know this, Andros?"

"What do you think I been doin' these nights? Twiddlin' my thumbs an' playin' mumblypegs?"

These were good men and tough that were pushing this fight for him, but suggesting they brace Reb Barstow's Half-Circle Arrow was asking a powerful lot. Barstow's outfit had its roots in the ground, and Barstow's name meant power the entire length of the Canadian. Andros could not blame these boys for pawing dirt; but he had to swing them round to it if he would see the Pool disintegrate. No other way was possible. Barstow must be smashed, his power made a thing for ridicule. Bocart had given this chore to him. Bocart was expecting results.

National Forests were the only answer to the two-bit rancher's problem, and it was this Pool that was blocking the government's efforts at every step. In this section Barstow and Red Hat were the Pool's chief agents. Red Hat was dead, but Barstow remained untouched. The Pool was beginning to breathe again. Shortly it would band its interests and stamp Andros' raiders into final oblivion—unless they smashed Reb Barstow now.

At that moment one of Kid Badger's Texans came in. He handed a note to Andros. "Lady at Rockin' T ast me would I git this to yo'."

Andros tore the envelope open.

> Come to the ranch right off.
> Grace Latham.

Rockinstraw read it across his shoulder. "I guess that Half-Circle Arrow raid is off."

Andros hurled the crushed paper from him. "Go get your broncs. We're headin' for Barstow's pronto."

Three nights later Andros sat glumly in a lonely cabin at the head of Alder Creek. The raid on Barstow's had been pretty much of a draw. Barstow's men had repulsed the raiders, had fought the flames and saved most of their buildings. Both sides had lost a few men. Andros' boys had gotten away with seven thousand head of prime beef, but the coup had fallen dismally short of the results he had hoped for.

His men thus far had scored many victories. The Southwest Lumber Syndicate was broken and bankrupt, its sawmills burnt and its men scared out of the country. Salmon Lake Basin had been freed of sheep; so had Horse Mountain and the Sierra Anchas. Asher's Basin had been retaken and the ranches northwest of Pius Draw had been reclaimed from syndicate riders and returned to their owners. Mormon Flat, the Tule Butte range and the Limestone Hills had been cleared of Red Hat's blatting flocks, and Tortilla Camp was strewn with dead sheep. Cave Creek Village, a sheep stronghold, was deserted. Pool interests at Sawmill and Schoolhouse Tank had been soundly thrashed. All across the country syndicate riders were quitting. Three railroad survey parties had been brought to a standstill and twenty miles of markers ripped from the ground. The Rincon was retrieved and Table Mountain cleared. Fifteen of Red Hat's Chihuahuans had been

151

killed at Apache Hill, and the syndicate ranches west of Curry Basin had all been gutted.

But this was not enough.

Against it, Red Hat's men had beaten them at Sombrero Butte, killing eight of Andros' raiders. At first Andros' successes had attracted other small ranchers to his side, but since that trap in which the sheepmen had dropped seven other of Andros' men—including the famed Sam Hackberry—no more owners had thrown their weight behind him. His money that Bocart had given him was gone—spent to the final penny. Red Hat's Chihuahuans had badly whipped the raiders at Pueblo and Sugar Loaf Mountain. Kid Badger had been killed in the raid on the Half-Circle Arrow and his Texans had promptly departed for safer places. New River Ned was down with a bullet in his groin, and Hernbarger and Obe Trane both were dead. The soldiers he had expected to come after that fight at Barstow's had not appeared, their officers no doubt bought off by syndicate money. Andros had counted heavily on getting those soldiers down here; their presence would have stopped all warfare and spiked the Pool's retaliation—which could be expected now at any moment.

Three weeks of blood and gore, and so far Andros could see the Pool was just as solid as ever. Its resources were illimitable. It was throwing hired guns into this fight three times faster than Andros' men could kill or scare them off.

He let his breath out in a dismal sigh. It had been a desperate hope, this play of Bocart's; doom-slated from the outset. He didn't blame Bocart for getting him into this. Bocart's back was against the wall, his hiring of Andros a final expediency. But the Pool was too strong for them; the two-bit ranchers had been right from the start. They had never had a chance to smash that outfit. They never—

He was like that, scowling, when a lean white hand flung the door back.

"Clem!"

It was Grace Latham's voice. He reacted to it sluggishly, the fatigue that was upon him showing visibly as he wheeled. His glance picked her up and it was not gallant.

"You don't have to eye me that way!" she lashed. "I didn't come here for myself!" Fierce strain lay across her features, reshaping them to a face he did not know. "It's Flame!" she cried. *"Flame Tarnell!* They got her yesterday—arrested her and carried her off—"

"What's that!" Three swift strides got Andros' hands upon her shoulders. *"What was that?"*

She grimaced at the pressure. But her eyes were level, frightened. "Flame's gone!" she whispered hoarsely. "I warned you something was up three days ago; I told you to come to the ranch—"

But Andros' grip was off her. He was whirling toward the door.

"Wait—*Wait!*" Grace cried. "I'm going with you—"

"No you're not! This—"

"Well, *I* am!" Art Rockinstraw stood in the open door.

"Then you better come a-smokin'!" Andros said, and whipped past him into the night.

25

WHEN A MAN FIGHTS

NIGHT was far advanced when Andros saw the lights of town. He came in sight of them alone, Rockinstraw's horse having gone lame and dropped him out of this six miles back.

With jaw tight clamped he passed the gaunted outlines of Long Rope's forgotten shacks. Light streaming from the batwing doors showed a pair of broncs standing hipshot before the saloon, and locust sound filled the gloom with jerky rhythm.

His saddle creaked as he swung to the ground. Skirting the broncs he went softly through the hock deep dust and, with an equal softness, mounted the steps. Floorboards skreaked as he crossed the veranda; another step and he was through the batwings.

Behind the bar Turly's head jerked up and all the color went out of his face when he saw who stood before him. They had the place to themselves. Andros leaned on the bar and hooked one thumb to his gun belt. "Never mind the rotgut. I'm not drinkin' tonight. I'm huntin' Barstow an' the sheriff."

Turly appeared to have trouble swallowing. He fumbled

a letter from his pocket and put it on the bar's gleaming surface. "For you. It—it come this mornin'."

His tongue made a frightened lick across his lips and he stretched his hands flat down on the bar. "Look! I—I ain't in this—see?"

"I never thought you were—"

Andros broke off as a man came in with his hat awry and his blue eyes popping. He did not appear to see Andros. He looked at Turly unbelieving and said: "Good Christ! you heard what's happenin'? They claim this thing's all over but the kissin'—they say the Pool's gone smashed all over! Busted! Beat! Barstow an' Red Hat riders is bustin' a blue streak towards the Border. Hossflesh can't get 'em out here quick enough! They say four of the Pool's biggest outfits is under the hammer—"

Andros' voice cut through to say: "Never mind the wild rumors, Turly—I'm wantin' Barstow an' the sheriff! Where are they?"

It looked like Turly had to prime himself to speak. "As Gawd's my—"

That much he said, and got no farther, stopped by Andros' lifted hand.

From the back room Barstow's voice came swearing—and a girl's voice said: "I won't! I won't!"

The bones showed up like castings through the skin of Andros' face. He left the bar, and the two leaning on it, and walked to the back room's door and opened it.

A lot of things came clear to him then; he understood what he saw immediately. *Krell wasn't dead!* He never had been! For there Krell stood against the wall, short steps removed from sheepman Duarte Salas. And a few paces nearer the door stood Barstow facing a scared-looking parson, his left hand tight-locked about Flame's arm.

But it was Krell that Andros watched. He saw Krell's muscles leap and stiffen—saw him take one backward, groping step. He'd have taken more if the wall hadn't been there. The wish was plain in his frantic stare.

"Clem!" Flame cried, and crushed the back of a hand against her mouth.

Barstow's ruddy cheeks jerked round.

Andros said cat-soft, "If you're ready, gents—" and let them finish the rest for themselves.

154

The parson groaned. Color was two wicked splotches on Krell's gray face. Barstow loosed an oath, big shoulders tipping. Salas stooped. He raised with the gleam of a gun in his fingers.

And still Andros waited. That had ever been his greatest danger—the weakness of this soft streak in him that would give every man the benefit of doubt. If the sheepman fired, the rest would slap leather. Andros knew that, yet waited for it stubbornly.

Then Salas fired, and the light went out in a shower of glass. Even as his guns slid clear Andros wondered why Salas had not sent that shot at him.

Then all was pandemonium, with lead ripping through this gloom and the thin wall rocking to the pulsing blasts as gun after gun made the smoke-reek fiercer. He saw the lean bright flicker of Barstow's pistol and drove three slugs in that direction instantly.

The neckerchief at his throat gave a jerk, something quick slapped his vest and his hat jumped back. He heard Krell yell, "Y'u damn' coyote, where are y'u?"— heard the smash of a slug biting wood beside him. He caught the scrape of someone's feet, and a long, shrill breath he could not place. A door slammed suddenly, and the muffled sound of Salas' shouting came to him from the alley. "Andros! Give 'em hell! I got the girl out here with me!"

Andros knew his safety depended on his staying where he was and holding his fire as much as might be till he got a definite target. No one would expect him to remain by the door.

So he stayed there. No sound came from Barstow, and Krell had gone cautious. Quiet crept among the dimming echoes—a hush so vibrant Andros dared not fill the empty chambers of his pistols. But he'd plenty left. He would make them do.

Then, abruptly, he could stand the wait no longer.

His left hand felt for the handle of the door. With a flick of the wrist he turned the knob. He took a long stride right and yanked the door open.

Light from the barroom showed Barstow down; he was over in the corner with his head between his knees. Krell was staring from the opposite doorway, lank and crouched, face twisted with hatred. He said, "I'm tired of yo' goddam follerin', Andros!" and jerked up his pistols to rake the shadows.

He was firing when Andros' bullet pushed a hole between his eyes.

Andros stepped across his body and lurched into the alley's coolness, pulling the clean sweet air deep into his tortured lungs. He keened the night with red-rimmed stare. "Flame!" he called. "Flame Tarnell—where are you?"

When no one answered he punched the empty shells from his guns and reloaded. He stumbled through this murk to the street. He stopped there, breathing hard. Flame stood by his ground-hitched horse. Lounging beside her stood Salas.

The sheepman elevated empty hands. "Nice evenin'," he said dryly.

"Salas, why didn't you gun me when you had the chance?"

"For why should I gun you? This thing is over—*es verdad;* the Pool is busted. Smash' complete."

"But why—"

"Quien sabe?" he drawled; gave a Latin shrug.

"I can't make you out," Andros sighed.

"Let it go like that." Salas grinned a little at Flame Tarnell. "I got a girl who is wait down below the Line. If you're through with me—"

"Go with God," Andros said, and shook his hand.

"Flame—" Andros said and stopped, at a loss for words to use with this girl who meant so very much to him.

But she seemed to understand. She said, "I know . . . Grace Latham told me after you had gone. She—she's going to marry Gallup John. Clem, somehow I can't help feeling sorry for her."

He nodded. "John'll be mighty good to her, though. I reckon he plumb worships that woman, Flame." He paused then, wondering how he was to speak his thoughts, to explain himself to her—to say what had to be said. Course the only thing he'd ought to say was "Good-bye"—and say it quick, but—

He had to find out how she felt.

"Guess I better be gettin' my truck together. If what's bein' said about the Pool is true, I reckon my job's plumb ended here."

She backed off from him, looked up at him anxiously.

156

Her lips seemed about to protest. Instead, they said; "Ain't you wantin' to ask me somethin' first, Clem?"

"My record's too damn' black!" he blurted miserably. "Besides, you wouldn't want me; I been married before! Krell—"

"As if that could make any difference!"

And then she was in his arms.

Minutes later he recollected the letter Turly had given him. He got it out of his pocket. Flame ripped it open for him because he had his arm around her. The document inside was very official looking. It was written on crinkly paper. It said:

Clem Andros
Long Rope, Arizona

CONGRATULATIONS! The National Forest Bill went through! You can name your job.

Cass Bocart.

THE END

157

Nelson Nye was born in Chicago, Illinois. He was educated in schools in Ohio and Massachusetts and attended the Cincinnati Art Academy. His early journalism experience was writing publicity releases and book reviews for the *Cincinnati Times-Star* and the *Buffalo Evening News.* In 1935 he began working as a ranch hand in Texas and California and became an expert on breeding quarter horses on his own ranch outside Tucson, Arizona. Much of this love for horses can be found in exceptional novels such as *Wild Horse Shorty* and *Blood of Kings.* He published his first Western short story in *Thrilling Western* and his first Western novel in 1936. He continued from then on to write prolifically, both under his own name and the bylines Drake C. Denver and Clem Colt. During the Second World War, he served with the U.S. Army Field Artillery. In 1949–1952 he worked as horse editor for *Texas Livestock Journal.* He was one of the founding members of the Western Writers of America in 1953 and served twice as its president. His first Golden Spur Award from the Western Writers of America came to him for best Western reviewer and critic in 1954. In 1958–1962 he was frontier fiction reviewer for the *New York Times Book Review.* His second Golden Spur came for his novel *Long Run.* His virtues as an author of Western fiction include a tremendous sense of authenticity, an ability to keep the pace of a story from ever lagging, and a fecund inventiveness for plot twists and situations. Some of his finest novels have had off-trail protagonists such as *The Barber of Tubac,* and both *Not Grass Alone* and *Strawberry Roan* are notable for their outstanding female characters. His books have sold over 50,000,000 copies worldwide and have been translated into the principal European languages. The *Los Angeles Times* once praised him for his "marvelous lingo, salty humor, and real characters." Above all, a Nye Western possesses a vital energy that is both propulsive and persuasive.